SECRET SERVICE OPERATOR #5 ™

AMERICA'S UNDERCOVER ACE

THE BLOODY FRONTIERS

By Curtis Steele

I0663414

POPULAR PUBLICATIONS • 2022

PUBLISHING HISTORY

"The Bloody Frontiers" originally appeared in the November/December, 1937 (Vol. 9, No. 4) issue of *Operator #5* magazine. Copyright © 2022 by Argosy Communications, Inc. All rights reserved.

OPERATOR 5:
THE BLOODY FRONTIERS

CHAPTER 1
EXIT FOR AN EMPEROR

THE AMERICAN encampment in Denver was dark—except for two splashes of light. One came from the many windows of American H.Q. in the Denver State Building, the other from the hastily erected, one-story prison where a former emperor brooded over his captivity. And the only sounds were the guarded challenges of sentries, as couriers came and went.

Over the State Building, once more flew the Stars and Stripes which for long months had been supplanted by the flag of the Purple Empire, whose victorious legions had swept across America. Now the mighty armies of Emperor Rudolph I were beaten back, and that same emperor sat tonight, a captive in a prison built especially for him.

His quarters had been well furnished, with soft bed, writing desk, easy chair, and a shelf full of books. America could be generous in the hour of her victory. And though Rudolph had not spared our women and children in his victorious march across the country, we thus far had treated him as an honorable prisoner of war.

Now, as he sat in his well-appointed prison room, a young man in a nondescript khaki uniform stood facing him. Though carelessly dressed, and showing the marks of sleeplessness and recklessly spent energy, there was yet something commanding about this young soldier that caused one to vouchsafe him a second glance.

Perhaps it was the poise evident in his bearing; perhaps, the

Jimmy's rifle barked five times in quick succession!

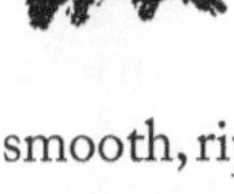

smooth, rippling strength that even the ill-fitting uniform could not hide; perhaps, the vital energy that shone in his eyes. Whatever the reason, one knew at a glance that this man was no mere private in the American ranks, and might have guessed that his nondescript khaki uniform could well have sported a gold star had he so desired.

And this was true. For Jimmy Christopher, otherwise known as Operator 5, was the man who had contributed most to the defeat of the Purple Empire. What is more, he was the man who had captured, virtually single-handed, the emperor he now faced.

HE STOOD at ease, speaking quietly, without rancor. "Rudolph the First," he was saying, "I am authorized by the American High Command to inform you of the disposition that is to be made of your person."

Rudolph remained seated, hands on knees, body obviously taut, under restraint. His thin, vindictive face expressed the hate that he felt for Operator 5. Small eyes bored into those of his captor's, and his lips curled in a sneer.

"Are you going to punish me for all the American women my soldiers raped? For all the men I crucified, and shot, and beat to death? For the cities I burned and leveled to the ground? Are you going to drop me into a vat of boiling oil, as I did to your people whom I captured in Pittsburgh?"

The emperor's eyes were shining with malicious triumph. "You cannot pay me back for all the things I have done to your country. You cannot do all those things to me. Had I won at the battle of the Continental Divide, I would have put every man in America to the sword. And you—you, Operator 5, would have lingered in agony for days, weeks—as long as I could have kept you alive and suffering!"

4

Jimmy Christopher's jaw tightened as Rudolph spoke. In his mind flashed those hideous pictures of maimed and tortured American citizens, victims of this mad emperor's sadistic love of the sight of pain and suffering. The urge was strong to put his two hands around Rudolph's neck and strangle him to death. He knew that Rudolph was not as brave as he sounded, for he, himself, had had the emperor at the point of his sword, and seen Rudolph throw away his weapon and cringe for mercy.

Operator 5 did not reply to that tirade. Instead, he proceeded with his message.

"The Continental Congress, now meeting in Chicago to form a new government in the United States, has jurisdiction over your person. They have instructed us to send you there under suitable guard. You will be given a formal trial, and your fate will be decided there. Prepare to leave within an hour. Your escort will be commanded by Captain MacTavish."

Rudolph's lips were still twisted in a sneer. "I will never be tried by your Continental Congress, Operator 5! I had two million troops under arms when you captured me. Those troops are still at large. They still acknowledge me as their emperor. Baron Flexner, my prime minister, escaped, and he is now organizing those troops. My navy is still intact off your Atlantic seaboard."

Slowly, he arose from his chair, assumed a regal pose. "I am still Rudolph the First, Emperor of the Purple Empire, Lord of Europe and Asia. Your country is ruined. Your resources are destroyed. You have no guns, no factories, no power, no light, no oil, no transportation."

He pointed dramatically to the candle upon the desk, which furnished the only illumination in the room. "See, you have become a primitive, backward nation. I, Rudolph the First, did that to you. But across the ocean, there is still a vast empire of which I am the master. There are huge armament factories, shipyards, vast stores of oil in Mosul and in Central Europe. Ships are being built, and armies being gathered by my faithful subjects in Europe and in Asia. If you dare to harm me, the whole world will march against you. And you cannot fight the world in your present miserable condition!"

Jimmy Christopher was silent, watching the other. There was bitterness in his heart, for he knew all too well that Rudolph spoke the truth. But he smiled coldly at the emperor.

"Nevertheless," he said inexorably, "you shall be sent to Chicago for trial by our Continental Congress. Be ready to leave within an hour!"

He went out silently, and closed the door behind him.

That door was made of iron bars—the only thing about the room that suggested a prison. There were many in the American encampment who held that Rudolph was nothing but a mad beast, who did not deserve this treatment. It had never been the American way to punish a man before he was found guilty by a duly constituted court.

IN THE corridor outside the barred door of Rudolph's room, a sentry stood guard, and in the lobby beyond the corridor there was a detail of five men under a corporal. The building had been placed at the south end of the city, away from most of the temporary residences which had been erected for the civilian population; for fear that the populace might become incensed by constant sight of his prison, and raid the place to lynch him.

Now, as Operator 5 walked away from the building, heading toward the State Capitol Building, where the American High Command was in conference, a figure detached itself from the darkness of some ruins behind the prison building, and stole silently across the dark intervening space, until it reached the shadows of the prison.

There was a moment of deep quiet, during which that shadow seemed to have disappeared altogether. Then, another figure detached itself from the ruins opposite, and darted across. A third figure began the quick trip, but just then the footsteps of the sentry clattered on the gravel walk. He was making his round to the rear of the building.

That third figure darted back into the ruins, and all was quiet except for the sentry's steps. The soldier came around to the rear of the building, whistling a tune. He was on guard for only another half hour, and he was thinking of the hot cup of coffee he would get when he went off duty. Coffee was getting mighty scarce, and it was rationed out carefully.

The sentry expected no attack, no attempt to rescue the emperor, for Denver was an armed camp, and he did not think that an enemy could enter the city.

Thus, when the dark figure rose up behind him, he knew nothing until the butt of a rifle cracked against the back of his head with wicked force. His skull was crushed in, and he fell without uttering a sound. He had paid the price of his carelessness.

NOW, AT a low whistle, other figures came running across the open space, until there were fifteen in all, gathered at the rear of the prison. Just above them, perhaps ten feet over their heads, the light streamed dully through the iron-barred window of Emperor Rudolph's room.

The moon came out fitfully from behind a cloud for a moment, and cast a pale gleam upon the scene. It illuminated the fifteen figures behind the prison, throwing its macabre light upon the Purple Empire uniforms they wore, upon the shining helmets, and the rifles.

Two of the men joined their hands, and a third, wearing an officer's uniform, climbed up onto their shoulders. Now his head was at a level with the window, and he whistled softly.

"Your Majesty!" he called, in the guttural language of the Purple Empire.

He waited a moment, and then the face of Rudolph appeared, between the bars. The man outside clicked on a flashlight for an instant, illuminating his features, then clicked it off.

Rudolph exclaimed: "Flexner! How did you get here?"

This man was Baron Julian Flexner, Prime Minister of the Purple Empire, who had managed to escape when Rudolph was captured.

Flexner chuckled. "Do you remember, Your Majesty, the underground tunnel that we built when we were in possession of this city? It ran from the Imperial Palace, under the streets, and out into that cemetery just beyond the city."

Rudolph nodded. "I remember."

"I escaped through that passage when you were captured, Sire.

It so happens that the tunnel runs directly underneath those ruins across the way. We entered it from the cemetery, and dug upward at that spot. I have forty men with me. Fifteen are here, and the others are hiding in the ruins."

Rudolph's face was pressed close to the bars. "You have come to rescue me?"

"Yes, Sire. I have been hiding with my men just outside the American encampment. We read their heliograph messages, and I discovered this afternoon that you are to be taken to Chicago tonight."

"That is true. But you cannot get me out of this damned American prison by cutting these bars. There is a sentry outside my door, and he looks in every fifteen minutes."

"We can remedy that, Sire. I have a dead American sentry here. One of my men will put on his clothes, and wait till they open the door to relieve him. When it is opened, my forty men will rush in and overwhelm the guard. Before the Americans from the city can come to the scene, we will be safely in the underground tunnel, and on the way out of Denver. They will never know where we went."

"That is good!" Rudolph's small eyes shone. "You have done well, Flexner!"

The Baron hesitated. "There is one other thing, Sire." He paused as if uncertain of his next words.

"Speak up, Flexner!"

"If we cannot rescue you here, there still remains another way. After all, we are only human. If we should fail—"

"Yes?"

"When we were defeated at the Continental Divide, your Chinese General, Shan Hi Mung, retreated with two divisions of his Mongol troops to Northern Illinois. He has received many thousands of Purple recruits from the disbanded armies as well as other thousands of your troops from Canada. He holds all of Northern Illinois, and the Continental Congress in Chicago does not yet suspect his presence. If we fail, and you are sent to Chicago, it will be simple for Shan Hi Mung to ambush the escort, and rescue you."

Rudolph's composure was returning, He stood up, squared his shoulders in the old pompous manner. "We shall not think of failure, Flexner. You will carry out your present plan—and trust that it shall not be necessary to use Shan Hi Mung and his legions."

Baron Flexner nodded. "That is what Shan Hi Mung said. He, too, is intercepting the American heliograph messages, and if he learns that you have started for Chicago, he will set the ambush. It will be impossible for him to miss you, as he controls every road into Chicago. He has captured every messenger sent there, as well as many of the delegates from the states to the Continental Congress. They are receiving no communications from the east, as they have no heliograph system there as yet."

Rudolph smiled thinly. "So Shan Hi Mung has a powerful force, eh? America shall yet hear from the Purple Emperor—and I shall make them dance to a terrible tune!"

"Shan Hi Mung proposes, Sire, that after you are free, he stage an attack upon Chicago. He believes that he could capture the entire Continental Congress while they are in session!"

"Excellent, Flexner! And now, proceed with your plan!"

"In a half hour more, Sire—as soon as the door is opened. Until then—I salute you!"

Flexner signaled to the men below, and they lowered him. At another signal from him, the balance of his force of forty men came out from the ruins and joined him in the shadows of the prison building. One of them stooped and began to strip the uniform from the dead sentry....

CHAPTER 2
A MISSION FOR A HERO

WHEN JIMMY CHRISTOPHER left Rudolph's prison, he made his way moodily across the city toward H.Q. He had a strange sort of premonition that something was wrong back there. Often before he had entertained such feelings, and generally there had turned out to be trouble. But he could not imagine anything happening. The prison was guarded by picked men, and there were several thousand American troops in Denver.

For a moment, he hesitated. He had an uncontrollable urge to turn back. But it seemed silly. He shrugged, and continued on. Just outside the H.Q. Building, he spied two familiar figures among the dozens of hurrying officers and privates. They were the figures of his twin sister, Nan, and her fiancé,

11

Captain MacTavish. It was the latter who was to take command of Rudolph's escort to Chicago.

Jimmy smiled as he saw them talking, their heads almost touching. Nan was dear to him, not only as a sister, but as a brave companion in danger. She, together with a small band of others, had fought side by side with Operator 5 through the trying days of the Purple Invasion. And he was happy to see that Nan had at last found a man she could love.

MacTavish was fully deserving of her affection. Formerly a sergeant in the Canadian Mounted Police, he had joined the forces of Operator 5 in resisting the Purple Invasion when Canada was attacked simultaneously with the United States. Now a captain in the American Defense Force, he had proved himself a brave soldier, though a bit bull-headed. He might have attained a much higher rank than that of captain had it not been for his recklessness. But he was a good man and a brave one, and Jimmy hoped that Nan would be happy with him.

He did not stop to talk to them, for he had important business to transact at H.Q. He entered the building, made immediately for a room on the main floor, the door of which was marked *Private*, and before which a sentry stood guard.

The sentry saluted, as he passed into this room. It was the conference room of the American High Command for the West.

Here, at a long table, were gathered the newly chosen governors of half a dozen states, as well as General MacPherson, chief-of-staff, together with a number of high ranking officers.

They greeted Jimmy gravely as he seated himself at the place reserved for him at the table. General MacPherson, who had lost an arm in the Purple War, rose and addressed him.

"You have notified the prisoner?"

Jimmy nodded. "He was vitriolic. The man is mad."

MacPherson shook his head. "Too bad we can't shoot him immediately. I won't be at ease until there is no longer a living beast like Rudolph. Captain MacTavish has his marching orders. He will call for the prisoner in an hour. Your sister, Nan, has requested permission to accompany the detail. Do you approve?"

Jimmy smiled wryly. "I wouldn't dare do otherwise. She'd go, anyway."

MacPherson returned his smile. "And now, Operator 5, we have another job for you to perform. As you know, the Continental Congress is meeting to elect a provisional President of the United States, to serve until we can bring the country back into shape. General Sheridan is the logical man for the job, and we want to see him elected. But there are a number of politicians already working against him. Several of the Western states have not yet sent delegates to the Congress, and we want to be sure to cast our votes for Hank Sheridan."

He paused a moment, then waved his hand around the table. "There are here present, the Governors of California, Arizona, Colorado and Oregon, who have the authority of their respective states to cast votes at the election at Chicago, which will take place in two weeks. They would rather not leave this territory at this time, and they wish to delegate you, Operator 5, to go in their stead and to vote for Hank Sheridan for President."

He glanced around the table. "Is my statement correct, gentlemen?"

The governors of the states mentioned nodded in turn. Each of them produced an official paper, which they passed around to Jimmy Christopher. "Those are your credentials, Operator 5. Since you know the country around Chicago, and since you are known to many members of the Continental Congress, you are the logical man to go."

Jimmy took the papers, and arose. "I thank you, gentlemen, for your trust in me. As you know, I have already been requested to represent the State of Nevada at the Congress, and I am going to Carson City for my credentials. From there I will go directly to Chicago. I estimate that I can make it in two weeks, with adequate relays of horses. I will leave tomorrow."

He shook hands with the various governors, and with General MacPherson, then left.

OUTSIDE, HE saw that MacTavish and Nan were no longer there. MacTavish must have gone to round up his troop to prepare for the trip, and Nan must have accompanied him. Somehow, as if by inner propulsion, he found himself directing his footsteps in the direction of Rudolph's prison. That premonition was still with him, and though it was only a vague feeling of unaccountable uneasiness, and he did not see what he could possibly discover by going there, Jimmy headed in that direction.

As soon as he came in sight of the building, he knew that his hunch was right.

It was just midnight, and the sentry was due to be relieved by the guard within. The sentry was there all right, but he was acting as no honest sentry should act. He was standing before the door, waiting for it to be opened, but he was paying no attention to the group of shadowy figures standing near him on either side of the entrance, out of sight of anyone who might open the door.... And all of those figures seemed to be holding short-barreled carbines, ready for action.

Jimmy, himself, had been walking in shadow, and he stopped stock-still, his eyes narrowing.

Somewhere in the city, from a belfry that had escaped destruction when the Purple hordes first took Denver, a bell pealed out the toll of midnight. Almost simultaneously, the door of the prison opened.

One of the guards from within stepped out to relieve the sentry.

And the shadowy figures on either side leaped upon the guard, felled him silently, and rushed into the building. Sounds of battle burst from within!

Jimmy Christopher drew his revolver, and ran forward, to within fifty feet of the building, and dropped behind a heap of stones in the street. He waited a moment, silent and grim-lipped, and then he saw some of those figures returning to the doorway, carrying candles to light their way. How they had gotten into the city, he did not know. But he knew very well what this meant. He rested his revolver on the heap of stones and rock in front of him, and fired once. The first of those leaving the building staggered, and fell back through the foyer, into the arms of his companions.

Whereas the sounds of fighting from within had been

comparatively quiet, Jimmy Christopher's shot echoed through the quiet streets like a tocsin. He fired again, and a third time, and each time he scored a hit. Bodies piled in the doorway. Now, a number of those figures, who had remained outside, began to return his fire, shooting in his general direction.

He moved around to the other side of the pile of debris, and fired three times more into the doorway, stopping another attempt to emerge on the part of those within. Then his fingers moved with incredible swiftness, as he reloaded.

The whistle of a military patrol was shrilling somewhere near-by now, and there were sounds of running feet. The alarm had been given.

SHOTS WERE coming at Jimmy thick and fast now, but he moved agilely from one side of his barricade to another, avoiding the slugs of those on the outside who were shooting at him, and yet managing to shoot often enough himself to keep anyone from leaving the prison.

He heard a voice from inside shout: "Escape, Flexner! It is a failure. Try later!"

He recognized that voice. It was Emperor Rudolph. So it was Baron Flexner who had executed this bold raid!

He emptied his second gun at the doorway, and turned just as a patrol came running into the street, led by a corporal.

Jimmy shouted to him: "It's a jail break! Sight on that door, and don't let anybody out!"

A second and third patrol appeared, and soon three dozen rifles were barking, hurling slugs into that doorway. Those within had moved back, and now no one was attempting to leave.

The figures on the outside of the prison had melted away, and there were no more to be seen.

An officer ran up with a magnesium flare, and hurled it into the doorway of the prison. It illuminated much of the interior, showing the dead bodies of those whom Jimmy had shot, as well as the huddled shapes of the surviving Purple soldiers inside.

Jimmy shouted to them in their own language: "Surrender, or we will charge you!"

After a moment, the Purple soldiers began to come out, with their hands in the air. The last to emerge was Emperor Rudolph.

Jimmy heaved a sigh of relief when he saw the emperor. He had thought that perhaps Rudolph had managed to get away.

Captain MacTavish, at the head of his detail, came riding up, all mounted, and ready to ride. MacTavish stared in wonder.

Jimmy looked up at him, and at Nan, who rode alongside him. "You almost didn't have a prisoner to take to Chicago!" he said.

Several of the American troopers had gone into the building, while others spread to search for those who had escaped. Soon, some of the searchers returned, to report to Jimmy. They had found the underground tunnel in the ruins across the way, but Baron Flexner and the men with him had already escaped.

Rudolph did not seem cast down by the failure of the jail break. Instead, he smiled in superior fashion. "You see, Operator 5, that I still have faithful subjects! They will never allow me to be tried by your Congress!"

Jimmy grunted. "Get him up on a horse!" he ordered MacTavish. "And start at once for Chicago. The sooner we get him there, the better I'll feel!"

He kissed Nan good-bye, and shook hands with the captain. "For God's sake, Mac, be careful. If you run into anything that looks suspicious, turn back. We can't afford to let Rudolph get free."

MacTavish grinned. "He'll get free—over my dead body!"

Moodily, Jimmy Christopher watched the troop ride away, with Rudolph mounted in the center. It would be a two weeks' trek to Chicago, and much might happen. He wished that the Continental Congress had not insisted on its prerogative of trying the emperor. It would have been better, he thought, if Rudolph could have been court-martialed and shot right here....

The next morning, Jimmy started for Carson City. He got his credentials there, and then set out for Chicago, only a day's ride behind MacTavish's troop.

He did not know that he was to overtake them sooner than he expected....

CHAPTER 3
AMERICA AMBUSHED

JIMMY CHRISTOPHER could see at a glance that the American detail was hopelessly outnumbered. He brought his panting, sweat-covered horse to a halt in the middle of the road, at the top of a slight rise. From here he had a perfect view of the straight highway which ran down from this hillock in a sharp grade to a narrow wooden bridge across a small river. Beyond the river was the burned, twisted debris of some large

JIMMY   CHRISTOPHER

city; and in those ruins the American detail had been trapped by the enemy.

Jimmy Christopher's lips tightened as his expert gaze took in the situation. The Americans numbered ninety mounted riflemen, under the command of Captain MacTavish. There were at least five hundred of the Purple raiders.

MacTavish had dismounted his men, and formed them into a hollow square, with the horses inside. They were kneeling now, and answering the withering fire of the enemy with steady volleys of their own. The Purple raiders were coming at them from all four directions, but they were not charging. It was apparent that they intended to rely upon their concentrated fire to thin the ranks of the Americans before coming to grips with them.

Jimmy Christopher swore softly to himself. MacTavish was making a bad mistake. Instead of forming a square, he should have thrown his detail into a flying wedge, and cut his way back to this side of the river. MacTavish was a fighting fool, but his mission this time was too important to warrant such spectacular tactics.

Jimmy Christopher bent low over his horse, urged the tired animal forward. His intention was to ride down that slope, cross the bridge, and run the gamut of the enemy in order to reach the hollow square. If he could make it, it might not yet be too late to change MacTavish's tactical blunder.

There was more than a mile of road between himself and the river, and as he raced toward the bridge, the air was filled with the crashing volleys of musketry, and with the sharp, vicious whine of snub-nosed bullets. Men in that hollow square were dropping faster and faster now, but the enemy troops still kept their distance.

Jimmy's heart thumped hard as he spotted, in the center of

20

the square, the prisoner whom MacTavish had been escorting to Chicago. Rudolph I, mighty emperor of the Purple Empire. This ambuscade had no doubt been carefully planned by the Purple raiders, to rescue their captured ruler!

Surely MacTavish must understand that there would be more Purple troops at hand, perhaps beyond the ruined city, to lend assistance to these attackers! Surely he must realize that the only course was to retreat and not to stand and fight! The rescue of the imperial prisoner must be prevented at all costs.

Rudolph had done enough damage to America, as it was. These ruins, among which the deadly battle was raging, had once been a thriving city. Now there was not a single building left standing. And throughout America, the same grim, dismal piles of debris and still smoldering ruins testified to the fierce savagery of Rudolph's conquering hordes.

EVERY FACTORY and mine in the path of the conquering horde was destroyed by the terrific bombardments to which our stubbornly resisting volunteer troops were subjected; and those manufacturing and mining areas which were not wiped out by the enemy were reluctantly disabled by our own retreating army, so that the Purple conquerors should not benefit by their capture.

As a result, now that we had decisively defeated the Purple invaders—largely through Operator 5's able direction—America was nevertheless reduced to a primitive state of existence. In all the land there was not an oil well capable of producing fuel for automobile or airplane; there was not a power plant capable of furnishing light or power, or juice for telephone or radio.

Everywhere, one could see abandoned autos, tanks, motorcycles, which could not be used, for lack of gasoline.

We were reduced to communicating by means of carrier pigeons and heliograph and smoke signals and fire beacons and we were compelled to depend for transportation upon the horse. Fortunately, there were approximately three and one half million of these animals extant in the United States at this time.* Fully half of these mounts were in the hands of the enemy, so that when the supply of fuel for automobiles, tanks and mechanized infantry gave out, both sides were evenly matched as to

---

* AUTHOR'S NOTE: Harrison Stievers, the noted historian of this period of American history, is the authority for the above figure as to the number of horses extant in the United States at this time. The reference may be found in Volume Eleven of his monumental *The History of the Purple War*. One can hardly believe that in the industrial machine age which followed the Great War of 1914, there were so many horses in existence. Yet, upon reference to some old almanacs of the year 1937, which were unearthed in the ruins of New York City Public Library, I find that this was absolutely true. One must realize that although almost everything was done by machinery in those days, there were still many thousands of acres of land which were still cultivated by the then-outmoded horse-and-plow methods. In addition, one must recall that the Americans of those days were fanatically interested in horse-racing and in the breeding of thoroughbreds. Those were the days in which the renowned War Admiral, offspring of Man o' War, set new track records, defeating such racers as Pompoon and Sceneshifter in the Kentucky Derby and the Preakness. Indeed, it seems to the author that Harrison Stievers might well have looked into the racing craze of the year 1937 and

cavalry equipment. After the battle of the Continental Divide, preceding years for some clue as to the reason why we were such easy prey to the warlike Purple Armies.

We recall that the decline and fall of the Roman Empire was facilitated by the easy, luxurious, slovenly ways into which the Roman citizens fell. Could one not look to the same causes in the United States of 1937? There are many points of similarity between America of the Twentieth Century and the Rome of the First Century. We, like Rome, were prosperous as a nation, though thousands upon thousands of our citizens were close to starvation; we, like Rome, had become soft through easy living and comfort; we, like Rome, had allowed ourselves to be lulled into a false sense of security—Rome had thought herself invulnerable because of her famous fighting legions, while we thought ourselves safe from attack because of the two vast oceans bordering our shores. Rome had grown soft upon expensive feast days, and glittering gladiatorial contests; we had grown soft through indulgence in luxuries, in gambling on horse and dog races (it had been estimated that in the year 1937, some thirty million dollars was wagered each day upon these races), and in pampering ourselves with autos and radios and motion pictures.

While dictatorships such as that of the Purple Empire in Europe concentrated every effort upon armament and upon the development of new and deadly machines of war, we concentrated upon frivolous luxuries. The result was, that when the Purple Emperor was ready to strike, we were not prepared to resist the might of his mechanized armies. Only when America was reduced to a vast stretch of smoldering ruins did the pioneering spirit which had at last been able to hurl back the conqueror. Now the sturdiness and courage of America was to be tested to the nth degree in the dangerous, back-breaking task of building the United States all over again, so that she the mounted groups of the Purple Armies had disbanded and spread over the land, forming into guerrilla bands which ravaged and harassed the countryside.

Some of them had taken possession of entire sections of the country, setting up small independent kingdoms and dictatorships under local war lords. One such band, consisting of three brigades of cavalry under the leadership of one of the Purple Emperor's most heartless generals—a Chinese known as Shan Hi Mung—had seized control of a spread of territory embracing both Dakotas, Minnesota, and a large portion of northwestern Illinois.

Thirty thousand hard riding, merciless Mongols, comprising those three brigades, had already put to the sword countless women and children in the seized territory, and were constantly raiding into southern Illinois, each time striking closer to Chicago, where the reborn United States had set up a *de facto* government.

Operator 5 could tell as he spurred his horse down toward the bridge across the Vermilion River, that the force now attacking MacTavish's detail was part of Shan Hi Mung's Mongol horde. **THE CONTINUOUS,** soughing whine of the enemy's Skoda carbines was almost entirely drowned out by the clean sharp bark of the pitifully few American rifles. Men in that

could rise, Phoenix-like, from the ashes of destruction. In a way, therefore, the Purple Invasion was to America, what the Flood was to the young world of Biblical days; it cleansed her, and wiped away the sin and corruption which had blossomed among us like a beautiful flower that was yet full of disease.

24

hollow square were falling faster and faster now, and the square itself was shrinking in size as the surviving men closed their ranks to fill the gaps where their comrades fell.

The end must come very soon now, and Operator 5 knew that he could do nothing to prevent it. The blunder had been made, and in war a blunder cannot be recalled; it must be paid for bitterly, in lives and in defeat.

Nevertheless, Jimmy Christopher urged his horse forward, down the road toward the bridge. He could now distinguish the tall figure of Captain Aloysius MacTavish, at the southeast sector of the square, with a rifle in his hand, fighting shoulder to shoulder with his men.

Desperately, impotently, Jimmy Christopher shouted to him, though he knew that MacTavish could not hear, "Make a break for it, Mac! For God's sake, make a break—"

His voice ended in a sob as he saw MacTavish fall under a hail of lead from the enemy's carbines. Now, the Americans were left leaderless, yet they fought on. Those men would fight until not one was left standing; Operator 5 knew that, and he gulped hard as he realized that those ninety men were doomed to die—every one of them.

By this time, Jimmy had reached the ramp leading up to the bridge, and he had been observed by the enemy as well as by the Americans. Shan Hi Mung's Mongols were wily, crafty fighters, and they must have realized that the Americans' only hope of escape lay back across that bridge.

And though they could see that Operator 5 was only one man, they must have desired to prevent reinforcements from reaching the detail. For, just as Jimmy Christopher reached the ramp, there was a dull detonation, and the middle of the bridge collapsed as if a giant hand had thrust down from the heavens against its timbers. The wooden span fell into the river below with a deep booming sound!

The road was closed to Operator 5.

Jimmy had been racing toward that bridge, demanding every last ounce of strength that his mount could give. And now, with the sudden blast, he was forced to rein in sharply, and to swerve to one side in order to avoid being precipitated off the broken timbers into the swirling river below.

A single Mongol marksman had swung away from the main battle about the hollow square, and he was kneeling on the other side of the river, waiting for Jimmy to pull up, in order to take a shot at him.

Jimmy Christopher glimpsed that sniper even while he fought his horse to keep it from stampeding. Out of the corner of his eye, he caught the man's tenseness, knew that he was about to pull the trigger of his carbine; and Jimmy did the only thing he could at the moment—he threw himself sideways off the horse, landing on hands and knees on the ground, just as the Mongol fired.

The shot whined harmlessly overhead, and Operator 5, working with the swiftness and accuracy which had often in the past saved his life in a tight spot, ripped the rifle from its sheath alongside the saddle-bags, and raised it to his shoulder. He hardly paused to take aim, but fired once, before the sharp-shooter could take aim a second time. His rifle barked, and the Mongol on the other side of the river threw up his arms, staggered backward, and then twisted grotesquely, to fall at full length on the ground. He was stone dead, with a ball through the forehead.

JIMMY CHRISTOPHER did not spare the dead man a second glance, but swung quickly toward where the main battle was going on. His lips tightened, and his eyes grew gray with pain as he saw that there was only a pitiful handful of Americans left—hardly a dozen.

And Emperor Rudolph I, the imperial prisoner, was making his bid for freedom. Rudolph had taken advantage of the fact that the Americans were too busy defending themselves to pay him any attention. His guards had turned to aid their comrades in the last stand, and Rudolph, left unwatched, seized the opportunity.

He began to run toward the Mongol lines, weaving a twisting course so as to avoid being shot in the back.

Operator 5's eyes became bleak. It would be an irreparable damage to America to let this man escape. He had wrought untold misery from coast to coast, and if he were once more at liberty, even though he did not have a mighty army at his command, he could be dangerous enough with three brigades behind him. And then, other divisions of his disintegrating armies, hearing that he was in the field again, might flock to his banner.

Grimly, Operator 5 dropped to one knee, and took careful aim with his rifle. This was to be an execution—and an execution that was fully justified.

27

The sights of Jimmy's rifle focused on Rudolph's spine. Operator 5 had never in his life shot a human being in the back. It was a thing he had never expected to be able to bring himself to do; but now he knew that he could do it. He kept the emperor in his sights, and his index finger slowly began to tighten on the trigger.

But he did not fire!

At the very moment when he was about to pull that trigger, another figure came into the line of fire. It was the figure of his sister, Nan. She was attired in khaki breeches, with a white blouse open at the waist, as he had last seen her in Denver. She carried a revolver holstered at her side, and a rifle in her hands.

As Jimmy, tight-lipped, lowered his sights, he exclaimed under his breath, "Nan! Oh God, Nan, come back!"

She was seemingly determined to prevent Emperor Rudolph's escape. But in so doing, she had interposed herself between Jimmy's rifle and the emperor, thus unconsciously saving the man.

Jimmy Christopher kept the rifle at his shoulder, watching his twin sister with anxious eyes. Her own rifle was apparently empty, for he saw her fling it away, and draw her revolver. He saw her shouting after Rudolph, and though he could not, of course, hear her words, he assumed that she was calling on him to halt.

Jimmy's heart was heavy, for he knew that Nan could never capture the emperor and bring him back across the river. His chance to shoot at Rudolph was gone now, for the Mongol troops, seeing that the Americans were reduced to a mere half dozen, were now charging at them, spreading out fanwise so as to half encircle them. This maneuver brought the Mongols between the river and Rudolph, so that Operator 5 did not have a clear shot at him.

The Mongols swarmed in upon the doomed Americans. And Jimmy shuddered as he watched, helpless to do anything, while bayonets flashed wickedly up and down. Then the bayonets were lowered, and the bodies of the last of the Americans lay, bloody and broken, under the wine-red rays of the setting sun. A gallant detail had perished because of a blunder; but the man who had committed that blunder was dead with them.

DURING THE last dreadful moments of the engagement, Jimmy Christopher raised his rifle, fired again and again into the thick mass of Mongols, picking off one after another, until his rifle was empty. Swiftly he produced more cartridges from his pouch, reloaded, while he kept his eyes glued to the other little drama that was being played out a few hundred feet from where the last of the Americans had perished.

Nan Christopher was running after Rudolph, who was zigzagging desperately. But she had gone only a few steps when a group of Mongol soldiers, under the lead of a burly corporal, bore down upon her with fixed bayonets, leaning far over in their saddles to thrust at her, while they spread out to surround the girl.

Nan was compelled to give up the thought of pursuing Rudolph, and act to save herself.

She swung around to meet the attack, and raised her revolver. The gun spurted flame again and again, as she kept pulling the trigger. Three, four of the Mongols were thrown from their mounts, and the rest raised their voices in mad shouts of vengeful rage, charging in at her with renewed fury.

Nan's gun was empty now, and she would have no time to reload. She would either be cut down ruthlessly by those flashing bayonets, or she would be taken prisoner, to be preserved for some diabolical torture which Shan Hi Mung would surely devise for the sister of the one man in the world whom the Purple generals hated most.

Nan faced the Mongols, her head held high. She was meeting her coming fate bravely, as Jimmy Christopher had always known she would.

But Jimmy had no intention of letting her perish there without interfering. His rifle was fully loaded now, and he fired swiftly, accurately, with a precision born of desperation and love for his sister.

The leading Mongol, closest to Nan, got the first slug through the side of the head. He pitched sideways off his mount, and the horse reared up, then pawed the earth almost a foot from Nan. Then Jimmy's rifle barked five times more in quick succession, and the remaining Mongols attacking her seemed to have been bowled from their horses like a row of ninepins.

For an instant Nan was free of attack. Looking toward the river, she saw for the first time the solitary marksman who had sprung to her defense. A glad light came into her eyes as she recognized her brother. But she did not waste time in waving, or in hysterics. Her thought reactions were almost as swift as those of Operator 5 himself, and she seemed to know instinctively what to do to take advantage of the short respite which Operator 5's accurate shooting had earned for her.

She seized the bridle of the horse from which the first Mongol had been shot, and vaulted lightly into the saddle. She swung the mount around, bent low over its neck, and spurred it toward the broken bridge.

Dozens of the enemy troopers saw the movement, and swung after her in hot pursuit, firing their carbines furiously. Jimmy Christopher had reloaded his rifle once more, and now he rested on one knee, coolly picking off the Mongols behind Nan. His shooting was so deadly and so effective that it slowed up the pursuit long enough for her to reach the bridge and clatter out upon it.

Her horse shied back as it neared the broken end of the bridge, projecting over the swirling waters of the Vermilion, but Nan put spurs to the animal, forced it to jump!

Jimmy Christopher held his breath for the space of half a minute while he watched horse and rider plunge into the current, almost disappear for an instant, then come to the surface and swim swiftly toward his side.

Behind Nan the Mongols had raced up to the river bank, and were firing both at Nan Christopher and at Operator 5 on the farther shore.

JIMMY DROPPED flat to the ground, stuffed more cartridges into his rifle, and shot methodically, accurately, at the men on the farther bank. Bullets were splashing viciously

Men and horses were mixed in wildest confusion!

about Nan and her mount in the river, and slugs whined close to Jimmy where he lay. But his own swift shooting disconcerted the enemy, and they lost heart at sight of their companions dropping under his uncanny aim.

They pushed back from the river bank, leaving a round half

dozen of their number dead on the ground. And Operator 5 seized the opportunity to reload once more. These were his last cartridges. He must make them go a long way.

Nan was in the middle of the stream now, and Jimmy caught his breath as he saw her horse swerve with the current and disappear under the water. Nan went down with it, and Jimmy uttered a choked cry. If the mount had been hit, Nan would find it difficult to disengage herself from the stirrups; she would be dragged down with it.

He watched, helpless to do anything. The Mongols on the other side began to utter shouts of fierce joy. They had ceased firing now, thinking that one of them had winged the escaping girl.

But in a moment their shouts of joy were turned to cries of rage as Nan's head reappeared, much nearer Jimmy's side of the river. Jimmy Christopher gulped.

"Good girl, Nan!" he muttered.

Now the Mongols were firing once more, but they kept safely away from the shore. They could still reach Nan in the water, but they were just out of range of Operator 5's death-dealing rifle.

Water splashed all around Nan as their bullets plowed into the river. But she continued bravely on, urging her horse toward the shore. At last she reached the bank, alongside the bridge, and Jimmy ran down to help her out. But her horse was able to find footing, and she cantered up onto the road, water dripping from her hair and her clothes, and from the horse's sleek body.

"Jimmy!" she cried, and flung herself from the mount into his arms.

He held her close for a moment, pressed her hard. "God, Nan," he whispered in her ear, "I thought you were a goner!"

Few people were closer to each other than were these twins. It was almost as if they could read each other's minds. And now Jimmy Christopher knew that his sister's thoughts were upon the dead body of her fiancé, Aloysius MacTavish, lying there where the Mongols had shot him, with the bodies of the other American boys who had perished so valiantly in the fight.

She was shivering in his arms, and he knew that it was more than her recent immersion in the river that made her body tremble.

"You've got to forget it, Nan," he said harshly. "You're only one of thousands. Countless women have lost the men they loved—husbands, brothers, fathers, sons. You've got to keep your chin up, and keep on fighting."

Suddenly, he pushed her from him, and pointed across the river. "Look at Rudolph!"

The Mongols had apparently lost interest in Operator 5 and Nan. Though it was possible for them to swim the river, they were no doubt deterred by the deadly shooting of Jimmy Christopher. And not knowing that he was down to his last batch of cartridges, they did not relish making targets of themselves by crossing the river.

Besides, there were more interesting things taking place on their side. It was this that Jimmy Christopher had noticed and called to Nan's attention.

Rudolph had been saved from Nan's revolver by the group of Mongols who had intervened. And now they were solving a problem that had been in Jimmy Christopher's mind for some time. He had been wondering why Shan Hi Mung should go to the trouble of rescuing Rudolph. The Mongol general was absolute commander of his three brigades, and if he should free the emperor from custody of the Americans he would be reduced to the rank of a mere subordinate, once more under the orders of Rudolph. But in the light of what Jimmy now was witnessing, Shan Hi Mung's purpose was made all too clear.

The emperor was being taken prisoner by the Mongols!

CHAPTER 4
THE MENACE OF
THE MONGOLS

A GROUP of the wiry soldiers were surrounding Rudolph, and two of them pounced upon him, pinioning his arms behind him, while a third began to bind him. The emperor struggled for a moment, but a Mongol officer stepped forward and struck him across the face.

Rudolph cringed from the blow, and offered no further resistance.

Nan Christopher was breathing fast as she turned to her brother. "Jimmy! They're taking Rudolph prisoner, after rescuing him! I don't understand—"

Operator 5 laughed bitterly. "It means, Nan, that America has a more dangerous enemy to face now than Rudolph has ever been! Don't you see? Shan Hi Mung now has the whip-hand over the disbanded Purple troops. He can force Rudolph to sign a proclamation ordering the various groups of Purple raiders to take orders from Shan. The Mongol general will make himself supreme."

The Mongols had remounted, and were forming into a column, to ride north. A small unit of perhaps a hundred troopers remained at the river bank, under command of a junior officer.

Jimmy nodded toward them. "We'd better make tracks out of here, Nan. That company is going to come after us."

Nan had managed to wring out her wet clothes as best she could, and now mounted, while Jimmy went after his horse. He joined her in a moment.

"Down this way," he ordered. "We'll follow the river bank. If we can shake those troops, we'll cross the river—"

"But why, Jimmy? That's enemy territory—"

He smiled grimly. "We've got to get to Chicago, Nan!"

For a moment she stared at him uncomprehendingly, and then suddenly grew pale. "Of course! The Continental Congress!"

If the Mongols were present here in Illinois in such strength, it meant that the Continental Congress of the new America was to be threatened with extinction. For if the Mongols were here, they could not be far from Chicago. And it was certain that the Congress did not have enough troops at its disposal to defend it from the ruthless raiders of Shan.

Jimmy Christopher's eyes met those of his sister. "We must get to Chicago as quickly as possible, Nan, and warn Congress. Even now, we may be too late. But we've got to try!"

Slowly, she nodded, then sighed. "Yes, Jimmy, we have to

try." Suddenly, she bowed her head. "Oh, why must we have this constant war? Why can't we have peace?"

She was interrupted by the crackle of musketry. Bullets whined about them. The Mongols had begun to shoot at them from the opposite bank of the river.

Operator 5 struck her horse's flank, sending it cantering away from the river. He followed, bending low in the saddle, while the slap of enemy bullets pursued him.

He glanced behind, anxiously. If the Mongols decided to cross the river after them, he and Nan would have scant chance of escaping, for both their mounts were tired and spent. And he saw that what he had feared was now happening. A detachment of the Mongols, under a wiry, long-mustached captain, was spurring into the water after them.

The fact that they should trouble to follow two individuals when they had just wiped out a whole American detail, and had accomplished their objective of getting the emperor into their own hands, indicated that they entertained some other purpose, in addition.

They would not be in a position to know that this man who had fought them from the opposite bank was Operator 5. They must think that these were just two Americans—and two unknown persons were not worth the risk of a whole detachment venturing into American territory.

What, then, could be the reason for wishing to prevent their escape? In a flash, the answer came to Jimmy Christopher. They must wish to keep the fact of their presence unknown to the

Americans. They wanted to prevent Jimmy and Nan from notifying American H.Q. that the Mongols were here in such force!

If that were the case, then Shan Hi Mung must be planning some major operation; and that major operation could be only one thing—an attack upon Chicago!

Now it became evident to him that there was much more at stake than his own and Nan's life....

HE WAS close behind Nan, and the Mongol detachment was gaining upon them steadily. The road ahead wound between two hills, with parched, long-neglected wheat fields on either side. If they continued along this road, they would inevitably be ridden down and captured. The Mongols must have realized this, for they had ceased shooting, and were riding hard after them, closing the distance between, little by little.

Jimmy shouted to his sister, "Keep going, Nan! We've got to hold our lead for a while longer!"

She was an expert rider herself, and she lifted one hand from the reins, signaling to him that she had heard. He smiled a little. His sister was game. She had just been through a terrific ordeal. She was sopping wet from her immersion in the river; she had been fired at, and had narrowly missed being killed. Yet she carried on as if she were engaged in a pastime instead of playing the deadly game of war, her life the stake.

Their horses' hoofs drummed in constant steady rhythm, and kicked up great clouds of dust from the dry road, so that it was almost impossible to see the pursuing Mongols.

Looking ahead, Jimmy Christopher saw that they were approaching a crossroad, perhaps half a mile away. Beyond the hills to the left, he knew, would be the Vermilion River. To the right, the hills fell away where the crossroad met their road, and in the open plateau there the government had planted a thick grove of pine trees in the dust-prevention campaign of many years ago. Those trees had thrived here, and now constituted a thick grove, in which a man might take refuge from pursuit.

Jimmy Christopher's brain worked swiftly in the emergency. Alone, he might baffle the Mongols. But with Nan—fine rider and good sport though she was—he would be handicapped. He saw clearly what the task before the two of them was now. Chicago must be warned of the close presence of the Mongols; and American H.Q. at Denver must also be notified, so that they could send troops to protect the Continental Congress.

He bent even lower over his horse, spurring it forward to catch up with Nan. She glanced behind, and he waved in the direction of the grove of trees.

"Make for that!" he shouted.

She nodded, and, when they reached the crossroad, she swung to the right, with Jimmy close behind her. He reached out and put a hand on her reins, slowing up both horses until they came to a halt. Half a mile behind, he could see the huge cloud of dust raised by the Mongol cavalry pursuing them.

Jimmy spoke swiftly, crisply, incisively.

"Nan, listen to me closely, and no arguments. We have to do two, things—warn Chicago, and get reinforcements from Denver. We'll separate here. You'll go west; I'll go east. Get to Denver as fast as you can, and come back with troops. Ride into that grove of trees, and go through it. Then circle back to the high road, and ride like the devil for Denver. Go by way of Peoria. General Malcolm should be there with a fair-sized force. If you meet him, bring him back. And before you go, give me some spare cartridges."

Nan's face was concerned, as she complied.

"But what about you, Jimmy? How can you get through?"

"Never mind about me," he said. "I'll manage."

"But—"

"That's enough, Nan!" he clipped. "There's no time for 'buts'. They're closing in on us. Get going!"

Nan Christopher hesitated a second, looking at her brother. She suspected that he was sending her into the grove so that he could ride the other way and draw off pursuit. But she had learned that in an emergency she must obey implicitly. She was a girl, but she had been brought up in a hard school. She had just seen her fiancé die before her very eyes; she had lost her father in the early days of the war; she had seen fathers, brothers and sons of other women give up their lives unstintingly for their country. Now, she could do no less than obey.

Her lip trembled. "G-good-bye, Jimmy. And for God's sake, take care of yourself."

He nodded grimly, leaned over in his saddle and kissed her. "Now, go!"

She reined her horse around, glanced back at the Mongol dust cloud, which had grown perceptibly nearer, and spurred her horse away toward the west.

Jimmy Christopher watched her go, watched her reach the

grove and disappear into it. Only then did he move. By now the Mongol troops were less than three hundred yards away.

HE UNSLUNG his rifle, saw to it that it was fully loaded, and then dismounted. He led his horse around so that it faced in the direction of the hills to the east, directly opposite the grove of trees where Nan had ridden. He slapped it hard on the flank, and it reared up, then raced away on the crossroad toward the hills.

The Mongols, sighting that dust cloud, raised a yell of triumph, and spurred forward with greater effort.

Jimmy Christopher followed the wake of his horse across the main road to where a gaunt, bare rock jutted out into the air. He knelt beside this, sighted his rifle upon the advancing detachment, and waited.

They rode toward the crossroad with wild whoops. Now he could distinguish individuals among them through the dust, and saw that they had slung their carbines into their saddles, and had drawn sabers. Their intention must be to catch the fugitives alive. Doubtless they hoped that the two captives would afford them some amusement over their campfire, when subjected to the cunning tortures for which the Mongols were famous.

Jimmy Christopher's lips tightened as he thought of the hundreds of American women to whom these same Mongols had done dreadful things, and of the men whose eyes had been gouged out with hot irons.

The Mongols were almost at the crossroad now, and Jimmy sighted carefully at the captain, who rode in the lead. He fired, and the man uttered a scream, threw up his hands. He was hit through the heart. The captain's horse reared up, and its rider slid off to one side, hanging by the stirrup.

Jimmy fired—five times more in rapid succession. His aim was accurate, cold, deadly. Five horsemen were hit, and their horses reared, swerved, while the Mongols behind rode into them, unable to stop. The detachment was thrown into wildest confusion, with riders striving to disentangle their mounts from the riderless horses of their slain fellows.

With swift accuracy, Jimmy reloaded, leveled his rifle, and emptied it again into the confused troop. Each shot was a hit, and the Mongols, demoralized, utterly in confusion, milled around, hopelessly entangled. Their very momentum, as they rode, had added to their discomfiture.

Jimmy quickly reloaded, but this time he did not fire. Instead, he darted out, directly into the milling crowd of troopers, and seized the reins of a riderless horse. He vaulted to its back, and, almost before he was discovered, was spurring away in the direction of the Vermilion River.

A few desultory shots followed him, but soon they ceased. The Mongols did not pursue him. Of the original twenty, there were less than half left, and these were without their captain. They doubtless preferred to return later, rather than venture, without command, farther into American territory.

Jimmy Christopher smiled grimly to himself as he topped the hill and came in sight of the Vermilion River. Nan should be able to get through to General Malcolm without much trouble. And if he could only reach Chicago....

CHAPTER 5
BALLOTS FOR THE BRAVE

I T TOOK fifty-six hours for Operator 5 to reach Chicago. He found every road guarded by Mongol troops. Twice he had to flee from large detachments of the enemy, and once he fought his way through a patrol. His horse was shot from under him, and he barely escaped capture by taking refuge in an old barn, which was all that was left standing of a once large and prosperous farm.

He stayed in the barn till nightfall, then stole out and walked four miles through the night to an enemy bivouac. He hit a sentry on the head, stole a horse, and continued his journey.*

It was midnight of the third day when he finally heard the

---

* AUTHOR'S NOTE: Due to the great amount of material which still remains to be included in these chronicles, I have been compelled to omit the details of Operator 5's adventures on this journey. But though I have devoted only two or three paragraphs to it here, there are four full pages of Operator 5's personal notebook which are crammed with the account of that trek. The desperate urgency which compelled him to push forward, without food, with a tired mount, and in the face of constant danger from enemy patrols, is vividly pictured in the notebook. This one sentence, taken from Operator 5's account, is particularly significant: "I struck that sentry from behind, with the butt of my revolver, without giving him a chance—and I hated myself for doing it that way. But I had to reach Chicago, for if the Continental Congress were wiped out, then everything that America had gained through a year and a half of sacrifice and suffering would also be wiped out at a single blow!"

welcome challenge of an American outpost in the outskirts of Joliet. It did not take him long to identify himself. He was given a fresh horse and an escort into Chicago.

The Continental Congress was holding a midnight session in the old Planetarium just north of Soldiers' Field, on the shore of Lake Michigan. The Planetarium was one of the pitifully few buildings of the city that still remained standing.

The young lieutenant who had escorted Jimmy Christopher to the entrance, said: "The Congress has been in session for ten hours now. They're electing a provisional President of the United States. Let's go in. I think we're just in time for the final vote."

Jimmy nodded, and followed him into the vast hall. The seats, ranging in a circle about the platform, were filled with representatives from almost twenty states. That platform had once been used to expound to happy audiences the mysteries of the heavens. But now, the great, complicated machinery, which had once reproduced the entire sky upon the convex dome of the planetarium, had been removed. Chairs were placed there, and half a dozen men were seated.

Jimmy, standing at the door, recognized Hank Sheridan, the thin, ascetic looking former small-town mayor who had taken up arms at the advent of the Purple Armies, and who had developed into a great military strategist. There were other prominent men upon that platform, their faces illuminated by the flares of torches which were placed in notches in the four corners of the big platform.

Other torches, located throughout the hall, threw a grisly light upon these proceedings of the Second Continental Congress.

GOV.
SLADE

NAN
CHRISTOPHER

HANK SHERIDAN
PRESIDENT

DIANE

TIM
DONOVAN

RUDOLPH

URSLUP,
THE STRONG

GENERAL
SHAN-HI-MUNG

Jimmy Christopher reflected bitterly that this congress was meeting under much worse conditions than that first congress which had met in 1776 to proclaim the inherent independence of America. This one had to contend with conditions which had been unknown to our forefathers.

The men of '76 had been fighting against a civilized enemy, and had had at their backs a young country, full of energy and resource.

This congress had to face the task of rebuilding a country that was now virtually razed to the ground, whose young manhood had been slaughtered by the millions, and whose resources had been destroyed utterly. In addition, we did not have peace after the war, for the millions of disbanded Purple troopers throughout the country were a far worse enemy than any organized army might have been.

Operator 5's attention was centered on the platform, where Major General Craven, the chairman of the Congress, was calling the roll. Apparently, they were taking a vote on the election of a provisional President, and, as Jimmy watched, Craven was calling the role of the states.

"New Jersey!" he called.

A secretary at the foot of the platform arose, and said: "The State of New Jersey is not represented at this Congress."

There was a moment of silence, and then the chairman: "New Mexico!"

Once more, the secretary arose and made the same announcement.

Major General Craven sighed. In quick succession, he called

the names of New York and North Carolina. Neither of those states were represented. Jimmy Christopher knew that delegates from all of those states had been sent to Chicago. They had no doubt been intercepted, captured or killed by the hordes of Shan Hi Mung's Mongol troops.

MAJOR GENERAL CRAVEN paused a moment. "Gentlemen," he said, "we know that the states whose names I have just called are with us in spirit even if their delegates are not present. I do not understand why they have not arrived. It is true that journeying is perilous in these times, but even if the delegations from one or two states have encountered misfortune, that does not explain the absence of the representatives of more than twenty states."

"However"—he shrugged—"I must go on with the roll call." He drew a deep breath. "North Dakota!"

A man arose from among a small group near where Jimmy Christopher stood. "North Dakota casts her twenty-two votes for Hank Sheridan for Provisional President of the United States of America!"

There was applause throughout the hall, and Jimmy smiled. Hank Sheridan was the logical man for the job.

"Ohio!" called Major General Craven.

"Ohio casts her forty-four votes for Frederick Blaintree for Provisional President of the United States of America!"

Once more there was applause.

Operator 5's lips pursed tightly. He recognized Frederick Blaintree on the platform, two seats removed from Hank Sheridan. Blaintree was a large, florid-faced man, with small eyes and a double chin. He was one of the old school of politicians, who had flourished in America prior to the Purple Invasion. It was men of his type who had spread corruption throughout the land, sapped our vitality, and contributed, in large measure, to the conditions which enabled a militaristic power like the Purple Empire to sweep across the land.

During the war, little had been heard from men like Blaintree. They had cowered in their homes, or else curried favor with the invader. But now that the Purple Armies had been smashed, they were coming to the front once more, using their wiles and eloquence to influence men again. And that those wiles were successful was evidenced by the fact that the delegates from a great state like Ohio were casting their votes for him.

There was a significant pause while the votes of the Ohio delegation were being registered. Operator 5 glanced around the great hall bitterly. The Ohio delegation were sitting not far from where he stood, and they all appeared to be smugly satisfied with the way the election was going. It was a pity, Jimmy Christopher thought, that men should so soon have forgotten the misery and suffering through which the country had passed, that they should be turning from honest thoughts of reconstruction to thoughts of politics and chicanery.

Those Ohio delegates were not inherently dishonest or bad men. It was merely that they were being led astray by the demagoguery and the eloquence of Blaintree and his associates.

The young lieutenant beside Operator 5 bent toward him and whispered in his ear: "This is the third vote they've taken. The convention has been deadlocked between Sheridan and

Blaintree. Sheridan polled one hundred and seventy-nine, Blaintree one hundred and sixty, and Osgood Smith, formerly senator from Ohio, got their forty-four votes. Now it seems that Osgood Smith has released his Ohio delegation, and thrown in his strength with Blaintree. That'll give Blaintree a majority, and he'll be elected President. It's too bad, because we need a man like Sheridan now."

Jimmy nodded. That need would be brought home to them a thousand-fold when he sprang his bombshell, and announced that Shan Hi Mung's Mongols were closing in on Chicago. But before telling them that, he had another job to do.

The Ohio vote was registered at last, and Major General Craven went on with the roll call.

"Oklahoma!"

Again the secretary rose. "The State of Oklahoma is not represented."

Craven appeared to hesitate. It was apparent that he hated to go on, knowing that the end of the roll call would see the election of Frederick Blaintree. But he had no alternative.

"Oregon!" he called.

The secretary was ready. Rising to his feet, he began the same routine announcement: "The State of Oregon is not—" He broke off there, his mouth agape. For the clear, cool voice of Operator 5 came from the back of the hall.

"I beg your pardon, Mr. Secretary. The State of Oregon *is* represented!"

The jumble of voices throughout the meeting room suddenly died away, and a pregnant hush pervaded, as Jimmy Christopher strode down the aisle toward the platform.

All eyes were turned in his direction, and now low whispers began to rise: "It's Operator 5!"

HANK SHERIDAN, sitting on the platform behind Major General Craven, recognized Jimmy, and a glad smile spread over his homely countenance. He half-rose in his seat, then subsided, raising a hand in greeting.

Jimmy Christopher smiled in return, and stepped up to the secretary, producing his credentials. While the amazed secretary examined them, one after the other, Jimmy turned to Major General Craven.

"Mr. Chairman," he said in a voice loud enough to carry to every portion of the auditorium, "while you are playing politics here, there is an army of at least thirty thousand Mongols closing in on you. By tomorrow they will be storming the outskirts of Chicago. This is a crisis greater than any we have ever faced. It needs a strong and courageous man to guide us. I have the honor to be the accredited representative of the States of California, Arizona, Colorado, Nevada and Oregon, and I am empowered to register the votes of those states at this convention. I hereby cast the fifty-eight votes of the States of California, Arizona, Colorado, Nevada and Oregon for Hank Sheridan for President of the United States of America!"

A steadily growing hubbub had arisen at Jimmy's announcement of the Mongol peril. Now, as he finished his dramatic climax, a great wave of excitement swept the hall, while the secretary arose and addressed the chair.

"These papers are all in order, Mr. Chairman. Mr. Christopher is empowered to represent the states that he has mentioned."

Major General Craven was smiling broadly. He realized that Jimmy's fifty-eight votes would give Hank Sheridan a majority over Blaintree, even with Ohio swinging to him. And others in the hall realized the same thing.

Blaintree was no exception. He saw his imminent defeat if he did not do something quickly. He sprang to his feet, shouting.

"I protest! This man cannot disrupt the proceedings in this fashion. I insist that the roll continue to be called. He may cast his votes for Oregon and Nevada, but he cannot vote for those states which have already been called and have not responded!"

Major General Craven seemed to be perplexed. He glanced down at Jimmy Christopher. "I've got to follow parliamentary procedure," he said. "If Blaintree insists—"

But relief came from another quarter. Jimmy's announcement concerning the Mongol horde had had its effect on the other delegates. The chairman of the Ohio delegation came to his feet.

"Mr. Chairman! The Ohio delegation wishes to change its vote. We had not realized the danger to the country. We are penitent for having thought to play politics at this time. In a crisis like this, as Operator 5 says, we need a strong and coura-geous leader, and not a politician. We therefore will now ask the secretary to change the records, and to register the forty-four votes of the State of Ohio in favor of Hank Sheridan for President of the United States of America!"

Almost immediately, another man in the body of the' auditorium arose. "I move a *vive voce* vote!" he shouted.

Major General Craven nodded to him. Another voice shouted: "I second the motion!"

Craven raised his hands to still the sudden outburst of enthusiastic shouts that echoed from the great rounded dome of the building.

In short order the motion was carried, and then came the *vive voce* vote. All of Blaintree's protests went unheeded. Everybody was getting on the bandwagon.

Hank Sheridan was unanimously elected Provisional President of the United States of America!

CHAPTER 6
THE PHANTOM PRESIDENT

A N HOUR later, Jimmy Christopher was closeted with Hank Sheridan—now President Sheridan, for in the press of the present crisis all formality and red tape had been done away with, and Hank had been immediately inducted into office.

They were both poring over a military relief map of Illinois, and Jimmy was marking in red pencil a rough line to indicate the probable position of Shan Hi Mung's troops.

"But what I can't understand," Hank said, "is why—if Shan Hi Mung has thirty thousand men—he doesn't attack at once. We only have half a regiment of Illinois Riflemen from Frazer's Fifth Division, and about two companies of Storm's Third Cavalry. We're in no position to offer any kind of resistance to an army of thirty thousand. And if Shan Hi Mung attacks before Nan can bring up reinforcements, he can drive us into Lake Michigan!"

Jimmy smiled thinly. "That's just what Shan Hi Mung doesn't want to do. He wants to capture the whole Continental Congress, including the newly elected provisional President. And I'd be willing to make a small bet that right now he's outfitting a fleet of boats of some kind, so as to bottle us up!"

Hank Sheridan's knotted fist struck the desk. "You've hit the nail on the head, Jimmy! What are we to do?"

"We've got to dig in!" Operator 5 told him. "We've got to throw up breastworks along the lake front, and dig trenches on the land side. It'll have to be a very small line of trenches, with the few men at our command. But we should be able to hold the Mongols off for a week. A week ought to be enough time. Nan has probably contacted General Malcolm, and if he marches at once he can hit Shan's rear while the Mongols are besieging us."

Hank nodded. "We'll do it that way. I'm giving you full command of all the available men in Chicago—"

He paused as a discreet rap sounded at the door. At his summons, it opened to admit an orderly. He was holding a tiny cylindrical tube of cardboard, which he extended to Hank.

"A carrier pigeon has just come in, Mr. President. It was carrying this message from New York, relayed over the carrier-pigeon system. The bird must have been shot at, sir, because there was a furrow in its breast that could only have been made by a bullet. Luckily, the shot only grazed the pigeon, and she came through all right."

Hank took the tube, and dismissed the orderly. He fingered the cylindrical message, and glanced at Jimmy.

"So the bird was shot at!" he said reflectively.

"That bears out my theory," Jimmy told him. "Shan Hi Mung is making sure that he cuts us off from every means of communication with the rest of America. He has every road guarded, and even attempts to shoot down carrier pigeons. That's why I couldn't get a message through to you. It's only by accident that this one came in. Let's see what New York has to say."

Hank Sheridan slid the onion skin paper out from the cardboard tube, and laid it flat on the desk, so that they could both read it. Jimmy's eyes scanned the hurried handwriting, and a low whistle escaped his lips. Hank Sheridan grew pale.

The message was as follows—

To the Continental Congress
Chicago, Ill.
Honored Sirs:

The Atlantic seaboard is in urgent need of immediate help. We do not understand why our repeated calls by carrier pigeon have not been answered. As we reported in previous messages, the entire Purple Navy, consisting of eighty first-class battleships, and more than one hundred light cruisers, sailed away to sea on the day that the Purple Armies were defeated at the Continental Divide. They were fully fueled, and completely armed. Those ships are now patrolling the coast-line, and threatening to attack unless New York capitulates. We need all available troops here on the Atlantic Coast. For God's sake, why don't you answer? Or don't you care what happens to us? This is the last appeal we will make. If it is disregarded, then God help America. We cannot!

> Signed,
> John Slade,
> Governor pro-tem
> New York State

SLOWLY, HANK SHERIDAN raised his hand from the onion-skin message, and the paper curled up. He lifted his eyes and stared in silence at Jimmy.

What remained unsaid between these two men was eloquent enough. They had fought for a year and a half, virtually side by side, each giving to the service of his country every bit of energy, courage and stamina in him. They had, by virtue of their unstinting service, seen their country awaken and rise up against the Purple invader, and it was largely by their efforts that America once more even had a congress.

But now, at the dawn of a reborn nation, when peace was so sorely needed to rebuild ruins and cure raw wounds, they were faced with perils from every side that threatened to heap new tinder on the still smoldering embers. All the work done, all the hardships endured, all the sacrifices made, seemingly were to go for naught.

At last, Hank Sheridan's lips formed the words, "It's no use, Jimmy. We're licked!" He smiled twistedly. "Here I am—me, Hank Sheridan—once the mayor of a small town, suddenly raised to President. A year and a half ago, I would have been proud to think that my tombstone, when I died, would remind the world that I had once been the mayor of my town. And now, I am the President of the United States of America! I ought to be proud and happy. Instead, I see myself only as the phantom president of a phantom country. It's too much for us, Jimmy. We used up all our resources in beating the Purple Armies at the Continental Divide. We can't fight any more. We can't fight the Purple Fleet. Don't you realize that, outside of that fleet, there isn't a big gun in the western hemisphere? That fleet could bombard us to its heart's content, and we wouldn't be able to fire a single shell in retaliation?"

Operator 5's lips were thin, tight. Inwardly, he half agreed with Hank Sheridan. But his voice betrayed no jingle overtone of the hopelessness he felt as he spoke.

"Look here, Hank. You and I have been through a lot together, and I can talk frankly to you, even if you are the President of the United States."

He got up from his chair, and towered over Sheridan, shaking a finger in his face. "I don't think you're a quitter, Hank. I know you pretty well. I voted for you for President, because I thought you had the guts needed at a time like this. Are you going to lay down on me now? Are you going to quit? Are you going to let the Purple Navy do what the Purple Army couldn't do? Or are you going to fight?"

He paused a moment, while Sheridan raised his head, a new light of courage in his eyes.

Then Jimmy Christopher went on slowly, *"If you're half the man I think you are, Hank Sheridan, you'll keep on fighting till you're dead!"*

Under the lash of his tongue, Hank Sheridan's shoulders seemed to straighten. His head came up. His eyes shone. "By God, Jimmy, you're right!"

He stood up, and his wiry old body seemed imbued with a strange fire.

"After all, I am the President of the United States of America. The people are looking to me for leadership. I can't fail them. And the worst thing that can happen to us is to die!"

"That's the stuff, Hank!" Jimmy Christopher breathed. "Now look here. You'll hold the fort in Chicago. Have trenches thrown up, and build breastworks along the lake shore. I'll get hold of some sort of boat here, that I can cross the lake in. I'll find horses on the other side, and get to New York. You do your part here, and I'll do my best to keep the Purple Fleet out of America!"

"It's a bargain, Jimmy!" said Hank Sheridan. "Wait."

He seated himself at his desk and picked up a pen, wrote swiftly. Then he handed the sheet of paper to Jimmy Christopher. He smiled wanly. "There's my first executive order as President of the United States!"

It was an order appointing Jimmy Christopher as Federal Commissioner for the Defense of the Atlantic Seaboard.

"I can't send them troops or guns, so I'm sending them you!"

Operator 5 stuffed the order in his pocket. "I'm leaving at once." He extended his hand. "Good-bye, Mr. President!"

"Good-bye, Jimmy," Hank Sheridan murmured throatily.

"We may never see each other again. But we can depend on each other to fight to the end, America is worth it!"

The two men shook hands, their eyes meeting in a silent pledge. Then Operator 5 snapped to attention, saluted, and backed out of the room....

CHAPTER 7
AMERICA AT BAY!

CHICAGO TO New York in five hours by fast plane! Those days were gone, as was the time when a stream-lined duralumin train could cover the distance in seventeen hours. It took Jimmy Christopher six days to get to New York; and it would have taken him much longer, but for the fact that in a little town in Ohio he found a garage where a small group of American patriots had hidden a hundred gallons of gasoline during the Purple Invasion. These patriots dug up a rusty motor-cycle with a sidecar attached, and in an hour it was cleaned up and adjusted, with enough gas packed in cans in the sidecar to get to New York.

That cut the remainder of the trip by about eighty percent. All along the route, wherever he stopped, Jimmy set up communication stations. He appointed men in each town to handle heliograph and beacon signals, and arranged a system of code by which they could relay messages. He sent out other men in every direction from these key towns, to set up other stations; and those, in turn, sent out others, so that in time there would be a network that covered the country.

Jimmy was able to see the result of these efforts, even while he traveled. He began to get reports from the stations already set up along his route. The news that trickled in from Chicago was not very reassuring. Shan Hi Mung had struck the day after Jimmy left. Hank Sheridan's hastily thrown up trenches had held for a day, and then the Mongols had driven the Americans back into the ruined streets of Chicago.

Just as Jimmy had predicted, Shan Hi Mung had planned to bottle the Congress up, cutting off their retreat by water. A horde of the Mongols had come down Lake Michigan on rafts, to attack the city from the lake shore. But the breastworks which Sheridan had erected along the shore kept the Mongols off.

On the third day after the attack, Nan had come down with General Malcolm. Malcolm had two divisions of Americans, and he had hit Shan Hi Mung's rear line. The battle had become a general one, raging along a hundred-mile front, and it had temporarily relieved the pressure against Chicago. What the result would be, no one could tell. Shan Hi Mung's forces were apparently even greater than had been estimated. It was thought that he also had under his command several divisions of Purple troops that had come down from Canada to join him upon hearing that he had rescued Rudolph.

With those additional troops, it was feared that he might be able to crush General Malcolm's two divisions.

At the places where he stopped, Jimmy Christopher tried to organize volunteer groups of men to march to Chicago to join Malcolm, but he found this very difficult. Thousands of men had finally returned home to wives and children not seen for a year and a half. They faced the task of rebuilding ruined homes, plowing barren fields, reshaping their lives once more to the changed conditions. And they were unwilling to leave so soon to fight again.

In addition, they had their own problems. For disbanded Purple soldiers were raiding everywhere, and men were needed to defend the homes and towns from these pillagers.

Jimmy gave up much needed sleep wherever he stopped, in talking to homesteaders and trying to convince them that the danger from Chicago must be met. If Shan defeated General Malcolm, he would sweep across the country, and no homes would be spared. A few men he did convince and several small contingents left for Chicago.

Jimmy, himself, did not know whether he was doing right in sending them. Perhaps he should have recruited them to march to the Atlantic coast, for the peril there was equally great. That immense Purple Fleet off our coast constituted an even greater menace than General Shan's Mongol hordes. And no news was coming from New York. He did not even know whether the fleet had struck yet or not.

It was not until he reached Buffalo that he really got a picture of what was taking place in the East.

HERE HE found men by the thousands flocking into the city to form once more into their old regiments and march to the coast. Everything was in turmoil. He learned that the Purple Fleet had struck once already at Washington. Admiral von der Selz, the commander of the fleet, had bombarded that city and driven away the American settlers who had come

in to rebuild it. Then he had landed a shore force and raided far inland, setting up recruiting stations where disbanded Purple soldiers could come to join him. As a result, he had filled his ships with troops, and was now somewhere along the coast.

No one knew where he would strike first, and, since New York was the center of reconstruction in the East, it was feared that that city would be his next mark.

Jimmy Christopher was forced to admire the strategy of von der Selz. The Purple admiral had not launched his fleet at New York at once, for he must have guessed that the Americans would concentrate their defenses there. Instead he had first strengthened his position by getting recruits, so that he now had an adequate marine force to put ashore after he had first reduced the city by bombardment. If he landed a few of the smaller guns from his ships, his landing force would be invincible, for the Americans had no big guns with which to oppose him.

Jimmy Christopher sat in at a conference with Colonel Brooks, the Commandant of the Buffalo contingent that was to march to New York. Brooks was more or less despondent.

"The boys have just come home from an eighteen months war," he told Operator 5, "and now they have to march again. They are asked to leave their women and children to the mercy of any raiders who may come down from Lake Erie, and they are asked to go and fight an almost invincible enemy. They're willing all right, because they know that if von der Selz is victorious at New York, their homes will be lost anyway. But what have they got to fight with? Rifles and a few grenades, against von der Selz's big artillery. It's a losing fight."

"Nevertheless," Jimmy told him, "we've got to fight. The Continental Congress is battling for its life at Chicago, and we can't let them down. Get your men started, Colonel Brooks. I'll be in New York before you, and I'll figure out some way to stop Admiral von der Selz!"

He left Buffalo, feeling not quite as confident as he had sounded in his talk with Brooks.

He wasted no time now, stopping only a few minutes in the larger cities, and going entirely without sleep. Long ago, in the Intelligence Service, he had trained himself to do without sleep for long periods of time, and now that training came in handy. By eating very sparingly, and by driving himself mercilessly, through sheer will power, he pushed ahead until he reached Passaic.

He found Passaic to be an armed camp, filled with American militia, under command of Colonel Killingsley, who had formerly been head of the New Jersey State Police, and whom Jimmy knew well.

Killingsley informed him that there were three thousand Americans under arms in the city, and that the Patterson Plank Road from Passaic to the Hudson had been converted into a ten-mile long stretch of trench system, manned by volunteers from Northern New Jersey and from New York.

Jimmy Christopher raised his eyebrows. "Why fortify the Patterson Plank Road?" he asked. "How can we be attacked from Northern New Jersey?"

Killingsley stared at him incredulously. "Do you mean to tell me you haven't heard what's going on here?"

"Of course I have. But I don't see how fortifying the Patterson Plank Road is going to stop von der Selz's marines. If the Purple fleet sails into New York Bay—"

Killingsley stopped him. "I see you haven't heard everything. Well, I'll give you some news. When Rudolph was captured by you, and when our army won the Battle of the Continental Divide, we attacked the Purple garrison here in New York at the same time. The garrison consisted of about four thousand men, but, in addition to them, there were three divisions of Rudolph's Gothic Infantry, which had just been landed here from transports. The Gothic Infantry was on this side of the Hudson, and they were taken by surprise.

"Well, they retreated to the Palisades, and they've been there ever since. They are practically primitive fighters, wearing leather breastplates and helmets. It seems that Rudolph recruited them somewhere in Upper Silesia. He let them keep their leather armor, and, in addition, gave them guns. They're cruel, merciless, half-savage men. They've begun to raid down here in Jersey, and often cross the river into New York. They staged a raid last week on a new settlement up in the Bronx, where we've begun intensive farming. They killed all the men, and carried off about a hundred American women."

Jimmy Christopher uttered a low whistle. "No wonder you're

laying down trenches. So besides having von der Selz's fleet to reckon with, we've also got these Gothic raiders at our backs!"

Killingsley nodded. "That's what makes it so hopeless. I'm sure the Goths are in touch, somehow, with von der Selz's fleet. When von der Selz steams into New York Bay, the Goths are certain to attack at the same time. We'll be taken between two attacking forces!"

Jimmy Christopher forced a grin. "You're not thinking of giving up, are you, Colonel?"

Killingsley swore lustily. "Hell, no! We've sent most of the women and children north into the wild country around Mount Vernon and New Rochelle, where they'll be comparatively safe. And the men down here are pledged to fight until the last one dies!"

Operator 5 nodded. "I told President Sheridan that we'd do our part here on the coast. And I think we will. I'm going on to New York. I'll communicate with you by the new code system. In the future, use nothing but code on the heliograph. I'm sure the enemy has spies everywhere, who have been reading all the heliograph signals. That's how they learned that Rudolph was taken to Chicago."

He left Colonel Killingsley, and got onto his motorcycle. In an hour he was in New York City, having crossed the Hudson by means of a rowboat.

CHAPTER 8
THE COMING OF THE GOTHS

NEW YORK was no longer the glittering metropolis that it had been before the Purple Invasion. She had stood the brunt of the first wave of the Purple onslaught. Bombardment had leveled most of her tall structures. The Empire State Building no longer reared her golden spire high into the sky, and Radio City was a heap of blackened masonry and debris.

Many of the streets gaped wide open where Purple shells had torn the concrete apart, exposing the intricate network of subway and sewer construction underneath.

Jimmy had brought his motorcycle over in the boat, and since he still had a precious supply of gasoline, he clung to it. But it was almost impossible to drive it through the city streets, due to their broken-up condition.

American militiamen were ensconced on the heights overlooking the railroad tracks which ran along the Hudson River. From where they stood guard, one could see the tall cliffs of the Palisades across the river, where the Gothic troops kept to their lair, awaiting another chance to raid. On the tallest peak of the Palisades there flew two flags. One was the familiar, grisly purple flag of the Purple Empire, with its sinister reproduction of the severed head and crossed broadswords—the flag under which Rudolph I had overrun the world. The other was the banner of the Gothic Divisions—a deep scarlet background upon which was emblazoned the figure of a huge Gothic warrior of some by-gone day. A leathern shield rested across his left arm, while, in his right hand, he gripped an immense mace from which dripped the blood of his latest victim.

There was a good deal of activity over there among the Goths, and Jimmy Christopher could see that hundreds of them were working down at the river bank, behind the protection of temporary wooden walls. These served to hide from view the actual work upon which they were engaged.

The heliograph had already flashed the news of Operator 5's approach, and Governor John Slade was waiting for him at the foot of Fifty-seventh Street. Slade was a tall, thin man, whose sparse hair revealed a high, scholar's forehead. He had been professor of military tactics at West Point before the Purple Invasion. He had also been a colonel in the regular army but suffered a chest wound at the Battle of Pittsburgh, early in the war. Now that he was unfit for actual combat, he was doing his best behind the lines.

He appeared glum, disheartened.

"I expected heavy reinforcements from Congress," he told Jimmy Christopher. "Instead, they send me only one man. This is America's weak spot. We must have our strongest force here, because, if the Purple Navy gets a foothold in New York, they can sweep the country—the way Rudolph did a year and a half ago. Does Congress expect me to bear the brunt of the attack, with the Goths at our back, when I have less than five thousand men available?"

Jimmy shrugged. "You forget that other sections of the country are in a bad way, too, Governor. The Continental Congress is threatened with extinction, and there are groups of Purple raiders everywhere. We have to be prepared with men at all spots where these raiders may strike. There's a good-sized contingent marching down from Northern New York, but I'm afraid that's all we can count on."

"Well," said Slade, "I'm glad that you're here to take the responsibility off my hands. It's too much for me."

JIMMY TURNED to survey the defenses along the Hudson. The city, at this point, ran along a cliff several hundred feet high, overlooking a flat strip of land below, which sloped down to the river. On this strip were railroad tracks, unused for many months now, and many landing piers.

Jimmy pointed below. "You haven't got any troops stationed down there," he said to Slade. "I see you've got them all posted on the Drive up here."

Slade nodded. "If the Goths should attack from across the river, I figure our men would be better off defending the heights up here, than on a level with the attackers down there."

"But that would mean," Operator 5 protested, "that you would let the Goths get a foothold on Manhattan without opposing them. From up here, you could never hope to keep them from landing!"

Slade shrugged impatiently. "Of course, President Sheridan's order gives you complete charge here, but don't forget that I was Professor of Military Tactics at West Point. I am not altogether unfamiliar with the methods to be used. Don't you see that if the Goths attempt to cross, our men could shoot them down while they were still in their boats. The range is easy from here—"

Jimmy Christopher interrupted him. "If you were the leader

of the Goths, what would you do—knowing that the Americans could shoot your men while they were still in the boats?"

Governor Slade's forehead wrinkled. "I would lay down a barrage with heavy artillery, to drive the Americans back from their positions, while my men landed—"

"You forget, Governor," Jimmy broke in, "that the Goths have

Squarely into the midst of the Goths, those cars charged, spouting flame and death!

no heavy artillery—any more than we have!" He did his best to keep from showing his impatience.

Slade was a good theoretical strategist, but, like all theorists, he buried himself in suppositions, forgetting the realities. Slade was still conducting the defense of New York according to the rules laid down by the War College in the days when warfare was conducted on a different scale. He had entirely neglected to take into consideration the fact that we were fighting with more or less primitive weapons, instead of with the scientific weapons of a year and a half ago.

Now, the governor appeared at a loss. "I—I confess," he stammered, "that I had forgotten that. But—but how could the Goths manage to land—"

"By building covered boats!" Jimmy told him. He pointed to the Gothic soldiers, working on the farther bank, behind the wooden walls. "Why do you think they're trying to keep us from seeing what they're doing? Because they're building boats with covered tops. Their men will be protected from our fire while they're crossing, and, when they reach this side, there'll be no one down there to oppose their landing!"

"By God!" Slade exclaimed. "I believe you're right, Operator 5! Lord, what a fool I've been! Let's give orders at once to move our men down to the railroad tracks—"

"We'll have to do more than that," Jimmy told him dryly. "We'll have to dig trenches down there. We can't have our men in the open, fighting the Goths in their covered boats. It would be slaughter."

Slade was visibly trembling. "Then let's get back to head-quarters at once. I've made my office at the General Post Office Building on Thirty-Third Street. I'll turn over complete control to you, and you can give the necessary orders!"

Jimmy Christopher nodded, and mounted his motorcycle. Slade had a carriage in which he had come, but Jimmy preferred to have his machine with him. He preceded the carriage, which was escorted by a detail of American cavalry. Slade was giving himself all the pomp to which he considered himself entitled as Governor of New York.

Mentally, Jimmy compared him to rough, simple old Hank Sheridan, who, as President of the United States, continued to live as simply as when he had been a small-town mayor. It was a measure of the comparative caliber of the two men. Slade was honest enough and patriotic. But he was simply not as great a man as Hank Sheridan.

AS HE rode downtown along the river front, Jimmy kept eyeing the opposite shore. The Palisades did not extend down this far on the Jersey side, and here Killingsley's Jersey Volunteers were entrenched. The Goths would have an easier time attacking New York City than in storming those trenches on the Jersey side. Killingsley was a practical soldier, and Slade, even though he had been a professor at West Point, was only a theoretician.

War, Jimmy decided, was no chess board, where men could decide involved theories of tactics. War was a cold practical business, where, instead of learning by a mistake, one paid for his blunders with his life—and the lives of countless others.

And suddenly, the short, quick *pops* of Jimmy's motorcycle were drowned out by a new sound. Drums began to sound along the river front, and a bugle's shrill notes rent the air. Almost immediately, rifles crackled, rolling up into a continuous crackle of musketry fire that seemed to cover the city with its dreadful crescendo.

Men and women in the streets began to run toward the river front, waving and pointing.

Jimmy Christopher brought his motorcycle to a halt, and Governor Slade's carriage rolled to a stop behind him. Slade came out of the carriage, and Jimmy joined him. Together, they stared toward the river.

The American riflemen were firing all along the line, across the Hudson. And Slade muttered an oath under his breath as he saw at what they were shooting. From the foot of those tall cliffs on the Jersey side where the Goths had been working, numerous long, high-powered craft were putting out into the stream.

Each of those boats was perhaps twenty feet long, and covered from stem to stern by a sort of roofed cabin. There were portholes down the sides of these cabins, from which protruded the long barrels of rifles. Below the cabins, there showed long, single banks of oars, by which the boats were propelled.

"Good God, Operator 5," Slade exclaimed, "you hit the nail on the head! The Goths are doing just what you said they'd do—attacking with covered boats!"

JIMMY CHRISTOPHER was watching those boats with narrowed eyes. Their bows were long and curved, like the boats of the Vikings of olden days. But these Goths had gone a step further, and protected the oarsmen and the fighting men by building cabins on them. There were twelve oars on each side, which meant twenty-four oarsmen. He estimated that the cabins must contain at least thirty men—making a total of more than fifty Goths in each of the boats.

The oars were flashing swiftly, in perfect coördination, propelling the Gothic craft across the river at a terrifying rate. Already they were halfway over, and the concentrated fire of the American riflemen, high up on Riverside Drive, was stopping them not one whit.

Now, many of the American volunteers ceased firing, and began to scramble down the slopes from the Drive, in order to meet the Goths at the riverbank when they beached. Jimmy Christopher groaned aloud.

"That's suicide!" he exclaimed huskily to Slade. "Our boys will be fighting in the open down there, and the Goths will be able to shoot them down from the protection of their cabins!"

Slade stared at the battle, white-faced. "Good God, Operator 5, it's all my fault! What can we do?"

The foremost of the Gothic ships had reached the shore now, and Slade pointed with a trembling finger. "Look at the flag on the prow of that boat! There's a gold crown on the flag above the axman. That's the ship of Urslup the Strong, chief of the Goths! He's the crudest of the Purple generals!"

Jimmy Christopher's lips drew tight. Urslup the Strong was the man who had led the Purple cohorts in the southern campaign against America. It was said of him that every night he went among the prisoners captured and selected a number whose backs he broke with his bare hands. If Urslup was in personal command of these Goths, then a dreadful fate awaited the inhabitants of New York. It would be better even to be razed to the ground by the Purple Fleet.

A second and a third Gothic ship now reached the shore, and the foremost of the American riflemen, having descended from the Drive, came charging across the railroad tracks in open formation to prevent their landing.

With perfect, ruthless timing, a deadly volley of rifle fire burst from those ships, sending a stream of leaden death among the Americans. They fell by the dozens, but the survivors kept coming on, firing as they ran. Their shots had little effect on the attackers, the Goths mowing them down at will. It should have been the other way around, for, since the Goths were the attackers, theirs should have been the task of running the gauntlet of American fire in order to land. But due to Slade's stupidity, and the Gothic cleverness, the roles were reversed. The Americans were bearing the battle's brunt.

The American riflemen had reached the railroad tracks, but they could not withstand the pitiless volleys cutting them down like so much chaff. They retired before those deadly blasts, and the Gothic landing party, now reinforced by others who had come ashore, swung into formation at the railroad tracks, and marched along the right-of-way toward the south.

And now, the first ship, with the flag bearing the crown, disgorged its quota of soldiers. In the lead was a huge, fair-haired giant of a man, whose leather breastplate was adorned with glittering stripes of gold, and who wore no headdress at all. In his right hand was grasped a heavy mace, and a long sword was strapped at his side.

Slade exclaimed: "That's Urslup the Strong! Look, Operator 5! He's leading his men south. They're not going to storm Riverside Drive at all!"

"Of course not!" Jimmy told him. "Urslup isn't going to waste men like that. He's going to march right around, and enter the city down here, where he can meet our boys on level ground!"

The Gothic ships were landing more men, and those which had already unloaded were returning to the Jersey side to take on additional troops.

Jimmy Christopher gripped the governor's arm. "Get back to your headquarters, Slade," he rapped. "Dig up all the reinforcements you can, and send them here. I'm going to try to stop the Gothic advance until you can get here!"

"But where will I get them?" Slade demanded. "I've got every available man posted along the Drive, up as far as Fort Try on Park—"

"Move them down here!" Jimmy snapped. "They'll do us no good on the Drive. Leave only a skeleton force on the Drive, and order all the others down here!"

"All right. But how are you going to stop them? Look— they're marching down along the railroad tracks now!"

Jimmy's eyes had swept along the strip of ground down there, and he had noted that two handcars were parked on the railroad tracks a block or two below them.

He gave Slade a little push. "Take my motorcycle. And leave your escort with me!"

Slade, a bit bewildered, obeyed, and Operator 5 shouted to the detail of Americans who had ridden with the governor's carriage. "Do you boys want to take a sporting chance on stopping those Goths?"

They had dismounted, and now crowded around him eagerly.

The lieutenant in command saluted smartly. "We're at your orders, Operator 5!"

"Good! The governor's going to move our boys from the Drive, down here to stop the enemy advance. We've got to hold those Goths up for long enough for the boys to get here. It may cost the lives of all of us, but it may save the city!"

"We're with you, Operator 5!"

"Then follow me!"

HE SET off at a run toward the railroad tracks, with the twenty men of the escort close behind him. The Goths were less than a quarter of a mile from this spot now, and advancing at the double-quick, with more of their men falling into formation behind.

Jimmy headed directly for the two handcars on the tracks. He reached them, almost breathless, and leaped up on one, tried the handlebars. They worked easily. He had been afraid that they might be too rusty for use. But obviously they had been operated regularly along the tracks—that being the only means by which heavy machinery of any kind could be conveyed, since the failure of the fuel and coal supply.

The two handcars were on separate tracks, and Jimmy split up the detail, mounting ten men on each. He, himself, climbed aboard one, while the lieutenant took command of the other. The Goths, seeing the small group of Americans on the handcars, began to fire, but the distance was still too great for effective aim, and the shots fell short.

"Forward!"

The men operating the handlebars bore down on them,

and the handcars began to move up the tracks toward the advancing cohorts of Goths. Slowly they gained momentum, as the sweating men at the handlebars kept them rising and falling with a continually increasing rhythm.

The Gothic column continued its advance along the right-of-way, with Urslup the Strong at its head. From the Drive above, the American riflemen continued to fire down upon the enemy, but they were, themselves, being subjected to volley after volley from the Purple ships in the river. The enemy ships were all concentrated at a point roughly about two blocks long along the shore, while the Americans up on the Drive were spread out thinly. Though many of the riflemen were descending to this sector, of their own volition, the bulk of them were too far up to be of immediate assistance. Most of the Americans, at the point of attack, had come down to repel the landing party, only to be laid low, so that the ranks of the riflemen here were pitifully small, while the Goths had already landed more than a thousand men, and were beaching more every moment.

It was against this powerful landing party that the two handcars, containing a total of twenty men, were moving.

CHAPTER 9
THE WAY TO WHIP AN ARMY

AS JIMMY CHRISTOPHER'S hand-car raced toward the advancing Goths, with the second car slightly in the rear, he crouched behind the metal front, beside two riflemen, peering over the top. There was a slight downgrade here, and the car gained momentum so that it seemed to be rushing at the enemy with the speed of an express train.

The flat strip of land here, between the Riverside Drive heights and the river, appeared to be full of Gothic troops now. Their column extended far back now. Urslup had thrown out sharpshooters at the right of the column, to direct a continuous musketry fire at the Americans up on the Drive, while he, himself, led the march south. In the meanwhile, under protection of the volleys from the boats, other craft were landing more and more enemy troops.

Lead was flying in every direction, and hundreds of shots clanged against the metal sides of the handcars.

Urslup apparently considered those two cars merely a laughing matter, for he continued his advance steadily toward them. With his huge shield forward, he resembled a real Viking of the ancient, savage days.

Jimmy Christopher reached out and took a rifle from the hands of one of the men beside him.

"I'm going to try and get Urslup," he said.

He rested the rifle on the metal front of the car, and sighted carefully, drawing a bead on Urslup's face, which was visible above the shield.

But the Gothic chieftain must have been warned by some sixth sense, for at that moment he raised his shield, and Jimmy's shot clanged against the metal, staggering the huge man for a moment, but doing him no injury.

Jimmy handed the rifle back to its owner, with a grimace. These were not the high-powered rifles of the Springfield type, which could have pierced such a shield without trouble. Our factories were no longer equipped to manufacture such weapons.

In a flash Jimmy realized that we had stepped back, in one short year, to the comparatively primitive existence of the eighteenth century. And we were moving back faster and faster. The leather armor of these Goths, and of the Mongol fighters of Shan Hi Mung might have been laughable in the days preceding the Purple Invasion, but it was becoming more and more useful as the deadliness of our weapons decreased.

Now the handcars were less than a hundred yards from the head of the Gothic column, and the wind was rushing past Jimmy Christopher's head as he peered over the top. The constant shooting between the American riflemen on the Riverside Drive heights and the Gothic sharpshooters had ceased. Both sides had stopped to stare at the audacious little group of Americans now charging head-on into the powerful column of the Goths in two little handcars.

From the center of the ring of warriors who were surrounding him, Urslup the Strong blew a shrill whistle three times in

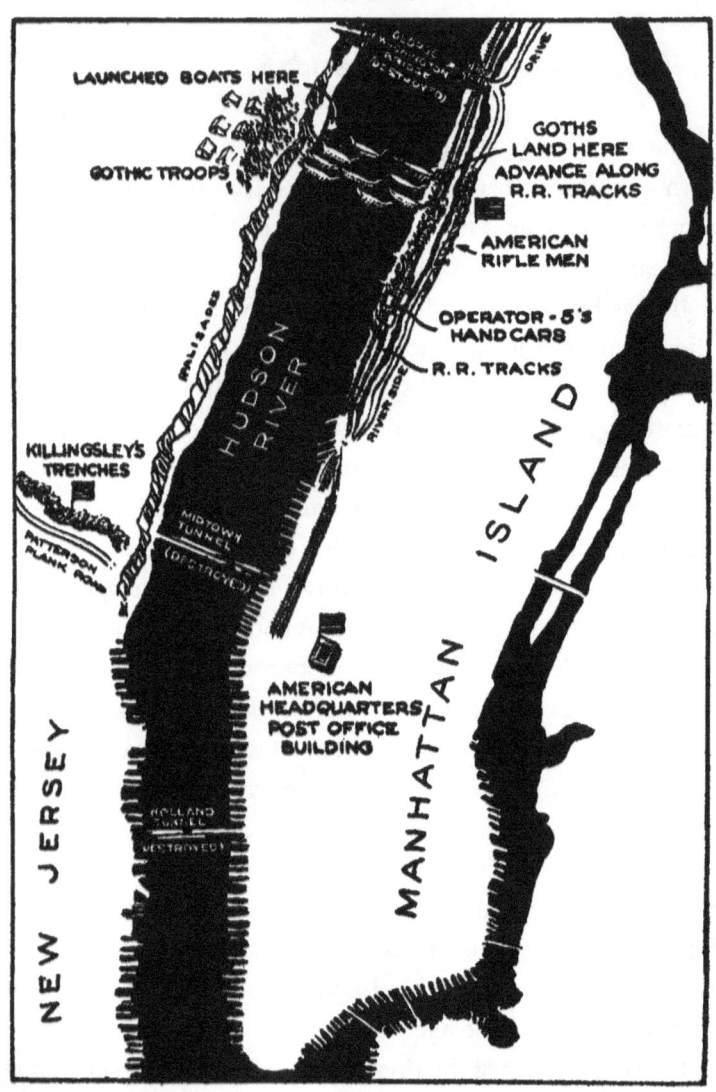

In order that the reader may better understand the nature of Governor Slade's tactical error, and the peril that faced New York, an outline map of New York City at this period is here appended. This map shows the positions of the Gothic troops and of the American defenders at the Battle of the Hudson River.

quick succession, and the column came to a halt. The front ranks dropped to one knee, and leveled their rifles at the handcars.

Jimmy Christopher shouted to the four men who were working the handlebars, "Get down! There's a volley coming!"

The four men dropped to their knees, but continued to work the handlebars from their cramped position. The car slowed up a little, as did the second one, in charge of Lieutenant Ferrara, but both cars continued to move toward the Goths.

The rifles of the Gothic troops spoke in a thunderous volley, and it seemed that giant sledgehammers were smashing at the sides of the little handcars. Again and again the rifles barked, and volley after volley clanged upon the metal. But these cars were built sturdily, and they resisted the hail of lead.

JIMMY CHRISTOPHER, crouching behind the front casing, raised his head over the top as the shooting halted for a moment. The front ranks were busily reloading their rifles, while men from behind were running forward to kneel and fire.

In that moment, between volleys, Jimmy shouted: "All right, boys! Give it to them!" At the same time he raised his hand in signal to Lieutenant Ferrara on the other car.

While the four men at the handlebars continued to propel the cars toward the enemy, the other Americans rose up, leveled their rifles and fired steadily, methodically, into the thick ranks of the Goths. Of the twenty-one men in the two cars, eight were working the bars, which left thirteen to do the fighting. Those thirteen rifles spat flame and death into the first rank of kneeling Gothic sharpshooters, cutting them down with unerring accuracy.

And now the handcars were almost upon the Gothic column. Reloading feverishly, the thirteen Americans poured hail after hail of lead into the Goths, as the cars sped through the scattering ranks of the leather-armored warriors. At this close range, neither leather breastplates nor metal shields were proof against bullets, and the Goths went down fast, scattering before the two diminutive Juggernauts that bore down upon them, manned by twenty-one courageous Americans.

Jimmy Christopher, using the rifle of one of the men at the handlebars, peered everywhere in search of Urslup the Strong. He knew these savage fighters, and he knew that if their leader were killed, they would be demoralized.

But Urslup the Strong seemed to have disappeared. Jimmy couldn't spot him, and he had little time to look for him.

The fighting was thick and heavy now. The American riflemen up on the Riverside Drive heights were cheering themselves hoarse now, echoing their cheers as they poured musketry fire down into the disorganized ranks of the Goths.

Now the cars had reached the far end of the Gothic column, having passed entirely through it. The rifles of the Americans were hot from constant shooting. Two men in Jimmy's car, and one in Lieutenant Ferrara's had been wounded. They were the handlebar operators, and others immediately sprang to take their place.

Jimmy shouted: "Back! Back through them, boys! We've got to keep this up for a while longer!"

He bent down, pulled over the ratchet that reversed the

cog-wheel, and the men bent to the bars with a will, sending the car backward along the tracks. Ferrara's car followed.

The Goths were attempting to re-form their broken lines, and the returning cars caught them flat-footed. The Americans poured lead into them, almost without retaliation, and the Goths began to flee toward the riverbank, where their boats were moored.

Jimmy gazed up anxiously toward the Riverside Drive heights. It was time that the reinforcements which Slade had gone to get should be here. But there was no sign of them. There were still only a few Americans up there, and those few began to climb down, seeing that the Goths were fleeing.

Jimmy groaned. This was the psychological moment when a small detachment of reinforcements would be enough to turn the tide of battle. Slade had failed him!

THE GOTHS at the riverbank seemed to be stiffening. Instead of returning to the boats, they were spreading to advance once more. And again the boats from offshore opened fire upon the American riflemen who were descending from Riverside Drive.

Operator 5 glanced out for a moment across the river, and a swift chill coursed through him. He saw now why Urslup the Strong had disappeared a few moments before. There was his boat, with the gold-crowned flag, being rowed furiously down the Hudson, and followed by the bulk of the Gothic boats!

Urslup had left this landing party here to engage the Americans, and he, himself, was leading an attack upon another section of the city!

Urslup was no fool. He knew that the Americans did not have enough men to protect every vulnerable portion of the New York river front, and was leaving enough men here to keep the Americans busy. It would be physically impossible to meet two separate attacks upon two different portions of the city. And since Urslup the Strong had plenty of men at his command, he could spread his front to outflank the American defenses.

But Jimmy was permitted only a moment to size up the situation, for the Goths were charging at the two handcars now, in open formation. They were firing as they advanced, and shots clanged upon the metal casings once more.

Many of the American riflemen who had descended from the Drive came running over to the handcars, but there was no room for them. Jimmy stood up straight, exposing himself to the Gothic rifle fire, and motioned to the American riflemen to take refuge in a string of dilapidated old freight cars that were standing upon a siding not far away.

The riflemen got the idea, and dashed for the freightcars, scrambling in as a hail of lead from the Goths followed them. This was what Slade should have ordered in the first place. There were enough freightcars down here to have provided barricades for all the American troops. They could have prevented the landing of the Goths from below, instead of spending their ammunition from the heights of the Drive, where the range was too long to reach the boats in the middle of the river.

The Goths were spreading out now, advancing slowly in such a manner as to encircle the two handcars. The Americans in the freightcars were directing a fast barrage toward them, compelling them to halt every few yards, and drop to the ground. Then the Goths would rise, rush forward, drop again. They were losing more men all the time. If only the Americans had used the freightcars from the beginning, the whole battle might have assumed a different complexion!

Jimmy Christopher saw that their position in the handcars would become untenable in a few minutes, when the Goths had them entirely surrounded. There would be no use in running the cars down the tracks once more, as they had done before, for the ranks of the Goths were not closed in now, and the thirteen rifles at his command could do little damage.

He therefore signaled to Lieutenant Ferrara, and shouted: "Evacuate these handcars! Take your wounded with you, and make a run for the freightcars!"

Ferrara saluted, and Jimmy ordered his own men to pick up the wounded. Four were disabled in his car now, and six in Ferrara's. It was all they could do to get them out under the enemy fire.

Jimmy Christopher was the last man in, and, turning toward the Riverside Drive heights, he thrilled to see a fresh contingent of American riflemen moving into position up there. Slade had finally come through, but, instead of sending reinforcements down here, he must have moved them into the heights commanding the tracks.

He slid inside the freightcar just as a fresh hail of lead swept into the wooden walls from the attacking Goths. They had seen the new contingent, too, and must have realized that they were now compelled to capture the freightcars at once.

Jimmy's car was crammed to capacity with men, kneeling near the open doors. As many of them as possible were trying to get a shot at the Goths. As fast as they emptied their rifles, others moved into their places at the open doors, thus keeping up a steady stream of lead.

This continuous volleying was too much for the Goths, and the leather-armored warriors began to fall back toward the shore.

But their retreat was cut off!

Urslup the Strong had now moved every one of the boats away from the shore, and all were setting back to the Jersey side to pick up more troopers. The landing party here must fight either until conquered or annihilated.

Now the Americans up on the heights, as well as those in the freightcars, directed a withering fire upon them, and the Goths spread out into even thinner formation, dropping flat upon the ground to return the fire.

JIMMY, WATCHING the course of the battle, was satisfied that the American riflemen would be able to hold their ground indefinitely. Now that the victorious advance of the Goths had been checked, and our boys had the advantage of the protection of the freightcars, there was little chance of the Gothic troops making much headway here. It was the flank attack, under the leadership of Urslup the Strong that Jimmy feared. He could see that all the boats were putting out into the river, heading south after the flagship, as fast as they took aboard new contingents of warriors.

And the flagship was heading in toward the shore, at a point about a mile south of them. Jimmy's eyes narrowed. That would be at about Thirty-third Street, where the General Post Office was—the building which Governor Slade was making his head-quarters. It must, therefore, be Urslup's intention to launch a drive against this point. Capture of the General Post Office Building would certainly cripple the American defense of New York City, and leave it without a directing force.

And there were no adequate defenses down there—*nothing*—to stop the landing of the Gothic troops or their march to the post office. The handful of officers and men who might be stationed there would be wiped out, and New York would become a great sprawling city without a head, at the mercy of the Goths.

Jimmy made his decision instantly. He swung about to Lieutenant Ferrara, who was in the same car with him. He had to raise his voice to make himself heard above the din of the musketry fire.

"Hold this position as long as you can!" he ordered. "If you let the Goths pass here, the city is lost. I'm going down to the post office. If any further reinforcements show up here, send them down after me, as fast as possible. Retain only enough men to enable you to hold the Goths!"

Ferrara's intelligent eyes sparkled. "You're putting me in command?"

Jimmy nodded. "I wish to God that a man like you had been in charge here from the beginning. Send a runner up to the boys on the heights, and tell them to send half their men after me to the post office. If they arrive after the Goths have landed, they're

Next minute, with fire licking their heels, they were hauled up!

to deploy into the streets around the Post Office Building, and go up onto the roofs of any houses that are still standing, or to take up positions in any cellars that they can find.

"They are not to stage an attack upon the enemy, but are to snipe at them, and endeavor to hamper their progress. Is that clear?"

"Right, sir!" Ferrara saluted. "And you can depend on us to hold the enemy here, sir. We won't let them come through and take you in the rear!"

"Good man!" Jimmy praised.

He shook hands with the lieutenant. "From the way you acted on that handcar, I'd say you will go far in the army—provided God spares our country!" *

---

* AUTHOR's NOTE: Jimmy Christopher's words were indeed prophetic, for this Lieutenant Ferrara, as many of our readers who are familiar with the history of the Purple Invasion will recognize, was the same man who later became Divisional Commander of the Twenty-seventh Route Army, during the Great Civil Insurrection of two years later, and who, because of his success in preserving the Union from the ravages of the Purple Kingdom in the Southeast, was elected Thirty-ninth President of the United States, succeeding Hank Sheridan. The well-known historian of the Purple Invasion, Harrison Stievers, says in Volume Nineteen, that Ferrara had been a comparatively unknown army officer, with no record to speak of, when he was elevated to the command of the Twenty-seventh Route Army through the intervention of Operator 5. Stievers apparently failed to connect the Lieutenant Ferrara of the Battle of the Hudson River, with General Sylvester Ferrara. But Jimmy Christopher did not forget that trying fifteen minutes

Jimmy moved over to the sliding door of the freightcar, which faced toward the city, and away from the shore. He waited a moment, while the men, under Ferrara's direction, set up a driving barrage to keep the attention of the Goths from the back door. Every man who could, crowded into the spaces before the open doorways, firing as fast as he could.

Jimmy Christopher waved to Ferrara, and jumped to the ground, running almost doubled over, toward the loading bins on the other side of the sliding. A few shots from the Goths pursued him, but he reached the protection of the loading bins safely, and swung around into Tenth Avenue, where he had left Slade.

Behind him he could hear the shooting fall off and become sporadic as the Americans settled down to the business of keeping the Gothic soldiers as close to the edge of the water as they could.

GLANCING TOWARD the south, Jimmy could see the ships of the Goths, heading in toward Manhattan. The flagship was not in sight. That meant that it must already have reached the shore, and must be unloading its soldiers, led by Urslup the Strong.

They would be attacking the post office before Jimmy could get there.

He looked around desperately for some means of conveyance.

on the handcars, when the young lieutenant commanded his car, and so ably followed him through the enemy column. The command of the Twenty-seventh Route Army was his reward.

A crowd of civilians had gathered here, and were watching the fighting. These were mostly old men and women, with a sparse scattering of children. A small group of them were gathered around some object on the ground, and Jimmy pushed through. He frowned as he saw the object they were inspecting.

It was his motorcycle!

He turned to one of the elderly men in the group. "Were you here when I left Governor Slade?"

The man nodded. "Yes. He didn't know how to use the motorcycle, so he got back in his carriage. He asked me to keep an eye on the machine."

Jimmy studied the man for a moment. He was in his middle sixties, stoop shouldered, with an intelligent face.

"What is your name?" he demanded.

"John Court. You're Operator 5. My son served with you at the Battle of the Continental Divide. He was killed there."

Court said it simply, but Jimmy could see the pain in his eyes. He put a hand on the man's shoulder. "I'm sorry. I remember your son. He was a captain in Buchanan's Brigade. He died bravely."

A speculative light appeared in Jimmy's eyes. "Look here!" he said suddenly. "Are you too old to fight? Are you too old to strike a blow to avenge your son?"

John Court leaned forward eagerly. "They told me when I went to volunteer, that I was too old. But by God, I still have a good fight left in me. And there are hundreds like me in the city, just aching for a chance. We've got weapons, too, that we hid when the Purple Armies first took New York. If you'd only give us a chance—"

"I'm going to give you that chance now!" Jimmy Christopher broke in. "The Goths are heading in toward shore near the post office, and we haven't got the man-power to stop them. Go home and get your weapons. Get all the men you can find who are willing and ready to fight. Bring them to the post office. I may not be able to contact you there, and you'll have to use your own judgment as to what to do. Don't engage the Goths directly, but try sniping at them from roofs and cellars. If I want you to attack them, I'll signal for the charge with four blasts of my whistle, followed by three short ones."

John Court was fairy trembling with eagerness and excitement. "God bless you, Operator 5, for this chance! Every man I can round up will be on the way inside of ten minutes. And if we can't do anything else, we'll at least have the same privilege of dying for our country that our sons had!"

There was a blur of moisture in Jimmy Christopher's eye as he gripped the old man's hand. He paused a moment, then said with the grave dignity which befitted the words: "John Court, by virtue of the authority vested in me by the President of the United States, I hereby appoint you to the post of commander of the Civilian Defense Corps of New York City, with the rank of captain!"

As the import of Operator 5's words impressed themselves upon Court, the old man straightened as if by magic, and a new vitality seemed to flow through him. He snapped to attention, and saluted smartly.

Jimmy returned the salute, and got onto the motorcycle. "Good-bye, Captain Court!" he shouted above the puttering of his motor.

The last thing he saw as he sped down Tenth Avenue, was the tall, straight figure of the old man, hurrying among the crowd to pick his recruits.

From back at the river front, he could still hear the desultory firing where Ferrara's men were holding the Gothic landing party. And from the south, from the direction of the post office, there came a new, ominous sound—the continual crackling of musketry!

The Goths had landed! They were attacking!

CHAPTER 10
THE FLAMING FORTRESS

A S JIMMY CHRISTOPHER raced southward in a desperate effort to reach the post office in time, he could see the heliograph on the roof of the Post Office Building flashing out its orders to the troops in the city. It was by that means that Slade communicated his orders to the American garrison, and now, Jimmy Christopher, who had trained himself to read Morse and International Code at a glance, could decipher the quickly flashing signals.

ALL AMERICAN TROOPS IN NEW YORK CITY
ORDERED TO REPORT AT THE POST OFFICE
IMMEDIATELY TO REPEL ATTACK. ABANDON ALL

POSITIONS, AND CONCENTRATE ON DEFENSE
OF POST OFFICE. CIVILIANS ARE WARNED TO
LEAVE THEIR HOMES AND TAKE REFUGE AT POST
OFFICE. THE UPPER CITY IS LOST.

Jimmy's hands gripped tightly at the handlebars of his motorcycle. Slade was forgetting entirely that if the Gothic landing
party were permitted to gain a foothold in Manhattan, it would
become impossible to defend the post office, which would then
be cut off from all supplies. He was giving way to panic at the
worst possible time.

Thank God that a man like Ferrara was in command up there
at Riverside Drive. Ferrara was soldier enough to know that
disaster would follow such a move, and he was man enough to
disobey that order, knowing that it could not come from Operator 5.

The heliograph continued to flash out its repetition of the
orders, and Jimmy Christopher gave his motorcycle the gun,
driving recklessly over the broken-up streets, circling open
manholes, and great gaping holes where enemy shells had
exploded. Miraculously, he avoided crashing, and at last came
in sight of the Thirty-fourth Street docks, which had been placed
in repair by the Purple Empire.

It was here that the Goths were landing and he could see
dozens of the enemy boats tied up and disgorging soldiers, while
others were already on the way back to pick up more men.

The Goths were marching in a steady stream toward the Post
Office Building, which was clearly visible from here, for no other
structures had remained standing between it and the river.

Brisk fighting was going on there, the bark of rifles and the wild shouts of the savage Goths filling the air.

Jimmy Christopher swung left on Thirty-eighth Street, and raced across to Eighth Avenue. Thirty-eighth Street was deserted, and he made good time across it, turning into the avenue just as a great blaze of fire burst from the front portico of the Post Office Building.

He brought his machine to a halt, and gazed at the scene, with cords tightening in his throat. Eighth Avenue was full of the leather-armored Goths. They were firing up at the windows of the post office, from which occasional shots came, from the rifles of the few American defenders within.

The doorways of the building, stretching almost across the entire length of the portico, had all been boarded up, and a storming party of Goths had made a dash across the street, under the protection of a barrage laid down by their fellows. They had placed kerosene-soaked rags and heaps of dried fagots against the boarding, then set them afire. The blaze was spreading, and soon the boarding over the doors would be burned away. Either the fire would spread into the building, driving the Americans out, or else the fire would die down, leaving the way clear for a storming detail of Goths to charge the post office. In either event, Jimmy saw at a glance, the Goths would achieve their end.

His mouth tightened into a thin line, as he watched. There was nothing he could do until the American reinforcements came up—and then it might be too late, for the Goths were landing by the hundreds.

Slade should have foreseen that the Goths would attempt to burn them out. He should have placed sharpshooters at all the windows, charged with the task of doing nothing but wait for just such an attempt. Even though the Goths had rushed in behind the protection of the wooden shield, it would have been possible for good marksmen to hit them in the legs, which would be exposed. That would have stopped the rush.

Now it was too late.

But someone in the building was going to try to put out the fire!

JIMMY CHRISTOPHER tensed as he saw a slim figure lean out from an upper window directly over the portico. The Goths were dancing about, holding their fire and waiting for the blaze to open the way for them. They did not at first notice that slim figure.

But Operator 5 did, and he groaned inwardly, as recognition dawned in his eyes. "Good God!" he muttered. "Diane! For God's sake, don't do it! It'd be suicide!"

That girl up there was one of the last persons in the world whom Jimmy would have wanted to see in a position of peril. Together with Nan Christopher and one or two others, she shared the affections of Operator 5, but in a far different way from his sister.

She was Diane Elliot, Jimmy Christopher's fiancée. Once a star reporter for a great press association, she had devoted herself to the task of fighting the warlords of the Purple Empire, side by side with Operator 5, hoping that some day peace would come, and permit the man she loved to devote himself to the business of making a home for her and him instead of risking his life for his country.

And Operator 5 could have found no stauncher, truer friend than Diane Elliot. Now she was going to almost certain death before his very eyes.

For she had dropped one end of a rope from the window, and in a moment was climbing down it, with a fire extinguisher strapped to her back. She was going down there under the enemy's guns, to try to kill that blaze! This time, Diane's utter fearlessness was leading her into a trap from which escape was impossible!

Now the Gothic troops saw her, and half a dozen rifles were raised. Shots *pinged* into the wall on either side of her, and one ball hit the fire extinguisher strapped to her back. The liquid poured down onto the fire, causing dense fumes of smoke.

Diane was only five or six feet from the bottom when she let go, and jumped to the portico, just clear of the fire. Jimmy saw her fall in a crumpled heap, and he thought that she was wounded. But in a moment she was up, one arm hanging limp. Something had happened to her arm in the fall; it had either been broken or sprained, or else she had been hit.

The fire was dying in spots where the extinguishing fluid had struck it, but it was raging elsewhere, along the length of the portico.

Diane staggered for a couple of feet, and the Goths set up a whoop, began to shoot into the fire.

The heads of a dozen Americans appeared at the windows above, and they looked down, as if to discover what was happening. They had apparently been unaware of Diane's attempt. She must have gone down the rope without telling any one, fearing that they would not permit her to go.

Now the Americans above shouted to her to grasp the rope. But she could not, because of her injured arm. She motioned to them to pull up the rope, but they left it there, and turned their rifles on the Goths, directing a steady hail of lead at them, in order to keep the savage warriors from shooting at Diane.

Jimmy Christopher had intended waiting here until the reinforcing troops came up. But he could not stand to remain here any longer, while Diane was down there, exposed to the fire of the enemy, and also in danger of being engulfed by the flames.

He swung onto his motorcycle, kicked it into life, and headed directly for the portico of the post office, driving straight through the thick of the Goths in the street!

IT WAS a moment or two before the Goths realized that this was no friend, who was speeding through their ranks. But by that time Jimmy had mounted the sidewalk before the Post Office Building. He had his revolver out, firing with his right hand while he guided the motorcycle with his left. He emptied the gun at the warriors in his path, and reached the portico. The Americans in the upper floors of the post office began to cheer when they recognized the khaki of the American Army, continuing their barrage to cover him.

Unwillingly, he abandoned the motorcycle at the steps of the building, and dashed up the stairs, toward where Diane crouched against one of the boardings which had not yet taken fire. When she saw him coming a glad light sprang into her eyes.

"Jimmy!" she exclaimed.

Her lips formed other words, but they were lost in the furious sounds of fighting. The Goths, infuriated at the audacity of Operator 5, attempted to storm the steps after him, but the fire of the Americans kept them back.

The tall figure of Urslup the Strong was evident, but he was not in the front ranks. As usual, he was surrounded by a body of his picked warriors, who would have to be cut down before he could be reached.

He shook his mace threateningly in the direction of the portico, where Jimmy Christopher had seized Diane about the waist.

"Darling!" he whispered in her ear. "You shouldn't have done it. There are plenty of men in there who could have tried!"

She smiled at him, resting in his arms. "I know, Jimmy. But I wanted to be doing something, too, while you were fighting the Goths at Riverside Drive. Slade told me what happened. If it hadn't been for spraining my wrist, I'd have been able to get up the rope all right."

Jimmy swung around, still holding her in his arms.

"I'm afraid that's the only way out for us, Di," he said grimly. "The fire is spreading. We couldn't go through it, even if the Goths weren't on the other side."

He lifted her high by the waist. "Get a grip around my neck," he ordered.

She did so, as best she could with her injured wrist, and Jimmy grasped the rope, wound his legs around it, and looked up.

The Americans, peering out of the upper window, waved to him, and began to draw the rope upward.

The flames were burning in toward the boarding, and the sizzling heat soared up at Jimmy and Diane, as they clung to the rope. And the Goths in the street opened an intense fire both at them and at the Americans above. Bullets chipped the masonry of the wall close to Jimmy's head, and suddenly he felt the rope slacken—then they dropped back to the portico.

One of the Americans at the window above had been hit, and had let go!

The jar of the short drop jerked Diane's arms from around Jimmy Christopher's neck, and she uttered a cry of pain, quickly stifled. Jimmy set about grimly reloading his revolver. If they were to be trapped, they would not die in the flames.

"I'm going to come out shooting, Di. You follow me closely. We may have a sporting chance of getting through them!"

Diane clutched his sleeve. "If—if we don't, Jimmy, remember—I love you!"

She reached up on tiptoe and kissed him. It was typical of both of them that they did not give way to despair in the face of almost certain death, but that they faced it coolly, and took the time to say an adequate good-bye, even with the flames of the blaze licking at them.

JIMMY TURNED to face the street, pushing her behind him. The Goths must have guessed that he would attempt something like this, for they spread out in the street, watching the portico like hawks.

Jimmy said: "We'll have to jump to get through the fire, Di. When I say, 'Ready', let's go!"

He waited a moment, was about to give the word, when suddenly a terrific outburst of rifle fire came from the windows above. A continuous blast of lead swept the street, and the Goths ran for shelter.

Diane plucked Operator 5's sleeve. "Jimmy! Look up there! Look what they're doing!"

Jimmy followed her pointing finger, and smiled. The Americans had evidently drawn every available man from the rest of the building to the front windows, and they were blasting the street to keep the Goths down while two of them pushed an aluminum radiator cover out of the window from which the rope hung.

From behind the protection of this radiator cover, the Americans were reaching out to grip the rope. They signaled to Jimmy to hitch on, and he once more lifted Diane so that she could get a grip around his neck. Then he holstered his revolver, wound his legs around the rope, and waved upward.

The fire was so intense now that they expected their clothes to take fire at any moment. And it was a happy sensation they had as the rope started its upward progress, bearing them away from the sizzling blaze.

The Americans continued their heavy barrage, driving the Goths back to the protection of the ruins of the Pennsylvania Station across the street. Many of the Gothic warriors fired at Jimmy and Diane from that refuge, and shots began to whine about them.

Jimmy clung hard, fighting to retain his grip against the added weight of Diane. Slowly, slowly, the rope lifted, bearing them up to the safety of that window. But before they reached it there was a blank space of wall to be traversed, and they were exposed to the marksmanship of the Goths.

Jimmy ducked involuntarily as a shot *pinged* into the wall alongside his head.

"You all right, Di?" he asked anxiously.

"Okay, Jimmy," she gasped. "But I feel like—like a clay pigeon in a shooting gallery!"

The fusillades of shots kept drumming deafeningly in their ears, and the bullets clanged against the radiator cover which the Americans above them were using as a shield. They were only a few feet from the window now, but that short distance looked like miles and miles of space. It seemed almost impossible that they should traverse that space without being hit.

They were sliding across the concrete face of the building now, upon which was engraved that famous legend which has served as a motto for the letter carriers of the nation—

"NEITHER RAIN NOR SNOW NOR SLEET NOR GLOOM OF NIGHT SHALL STAY THESE COURIERS FROM THE SWIFT COMPLETION OF THEIR APPOINTED ROUNDS."

It is strange what a man will think of while he is hanging between life and death. Jimmy Christopher could not talk to Diane now, because he could not have made himself heard above the uproar of the battle. But he felt her warm body quivering as she clung close to him, and he thought of the thousands of "swift couriers" who would never complete their rounds again—men who had fought for America against the cruelty and terror of the Purple Invasion, just as these Americans here in the Post Office Building were fighting against the onslaught of the Goths. It had indeed taken more than "rain or snow or sleet or gloom of night" to stay them from the completion of their appointed rounds. It had taken a cataclysm like the Purple Invasion. And Jimmy Christopher wondered, as he hung by that slowly rising rope, if there would ever again be a mail service in the United States—if there would ever be a United States again, for that matter!

They were close to the window above them now, and the Americans, in their anxiety to haul up the rope, let go of the radiator cover. It fell past Jimmy and Diane, brushing them, and down into the flames below.

The Goths raised a shout to see the protection gone from the men at the rope, and renewed the intensity of their shooting. The Americans, from all the windows along the front of the building, increased their fire as well, driving the Goths back to cover, and spoiling their marksmanship.

How Jimmy and Diane escaped being hit on that perilous ascent is more than Jimmy could ever understand. But some guardian angel, who had seemed to provide him with a charmed life throughout the dangerous days of the Purple Invasion must have continued its good offices. For they both reached that window unhit, and eager hands reached out to pull Diane in. Jimmy climbed in after her swiftly, and almost fell into the arms of a small, wiry boy of perhaps fifteen who was almost crying with joy.

Operator 5 exclaimed: "Tim! Tim Donovan! What are you doing here?"

The boy was pawing him all over to see if he were wounded. "Gosh, Jimmy, I sure thought you and Diane were hit. The shots were flying so thick around you, I don't see how you escaped!"

Tim Donovan was a freckle-faced Irish lad who had attached himself to Operator 5 a couple of years ago. At that time, the Irish lad had rendered Jimmy Christopher a signal service, and Jimmy had taken him under his wing, teaching him to do many things that grown men would have envied. As a result, Tim Donovan, though too young to qualify for the Intelligence Service, had become an able but unofficial assistant of Operator 5.

"I came here with Diane," the boy explained, "when we heard you were on the way to New York. If I had seen Diane trying that crazy stunt with the fire extinguisher, I would have tied her up!"

Governor Slade came into the room, pale, with dark shadows under his eyes.

"Operator 5," he said, "I've made a fizzle of this whole thing. For God's sake, take over. I don't think anybody can get out of this mess now!"

Operator 5 put a hand on his shoulder. "Nobody's blaming you, Governor. You did the best that you knew how."

CHAPTER 11
HOT WATER FOR VANDALS

HE SWUNG to the window, and saw that the Goths were coming out of the ruins of Pennsylvania Station across the street, in open formation, preparing to charge the portico. He put his head out of the window, and saw that the fire had gained headway. Though he could not see the boardings across the doors from the window, he guessed that they must be partially burned away by this time. The building was of fireproof construction, and, as soon as the boardings were gone, the fire would naturally die down because of lack of anything to feed upon. And that would be the cue for the Goths to charge.

Jimmy turned back to Slade. "Have you any water supply?" he demanded.

Slade nodded. "A water tower was erected on the roof of the building, when the city water supply failed."

"How about hose?"

Slade looked doubtful, but one of the American riflemen interjected, "There's plenty of hose down in the cellar, Operator 5. I saw it when I went down for ammunition."

"Good!" said Jimmy. "Get a dozen men. Bring up fifty feet of hose and connect it in two lines to the water tower. See that the nozzles reach to the hall opposite the front doors."

The riflemen saluted, and went to obey the order.

Tim Donovan and Diane looked at Jimmy questioningly. He smiled at them.

Operator 5 and Urslup the Strong faced each other—

chieftain against chieftain, in a battle to the death.

"We'll arrange a little welcome for the Goths when they charge."

Once more he looked out the window, peering far down the

street, in spite of the hail of bullets that met his appearance. He was looking for the reinforcements that he had ordered. And sure enough, about two blocks down he spied a straggling column of Americans, deploying into Eighth Avenue from one of the side streets.

That would be Court and the old men whom he had recruited.

As he watched, he saw those old men melt away into the debris of the buildings that lined the avenue, disappearing by twos and threes. John Court was obeying Jimmy's order not to attack the Goths until he received the signal.

From the west, where the Goths were still disembarking from their ships, Jimmy could hear the sounds of sporadic shooting. That would be the regular American riflemen who had moved down from Riverside Drive. Their orders had been to take up positions on roofs and in cellars, and to endeavor to impede the progress of the Goths into the city, by sniping.

Jimmy drew in his head, and nodded with satisfaction to Tim and Diane.

"The stage is set," he told them. "We're going to make our big try in a couple of minutes. The next quarter of an hour will tell whether New York remains free, or falls to the mercy of the Goths!"

The rifleman who had gone down to attend to the hose came into the room. "Everything is ready, Operator 5," he reported. "The hose is hooked up to the water tower, and two nozzles are fixed opposite the front doors. I've got six men on each nozzle. We'll need that many, because I figure that we can develop about seventy-five pounds pressure in each hose."

"Fine!" Jimmy approved. "Now if we could only get that water piping hot—"

The rifleman interrupted, grinning broadly. "I figured you'd want something like that, Operator 5, so I had them start the furnaces downstairs. We broke up all the chairs and tables we could find, and we've got the furnaces going strong. When that water comes out of the nozzles, it'll be scalding!"

"Good man!" said Jimmy. "What's your name?"

"Peter Flanagan, sir."

"All right, Flanagan. You take charge of the hose crew down there. Don't let go until I give the signal—four long blasts, followed by three short ones."

Flanagan saluted and left.

Jimmy swung around, issuing swift orders. "I want fifty riflemen down there in the hall, ready for orders. I want every other man with a gun to take a station at the windows. No shooting now. Let the Goths come right up into the portico. Start firing when you get the signal!"

He turned to Diane Elliot and Tim Donovan. "Diane, you and Tim take charge of the rear of the building. The Goths haven't made any attempts there, and I think they'll stage one now, simultaneously with the charge at the front door. It'll be harder for them to gain their objective there, because the street in back of this building is caved in. And the riflemen from Riverside Drive must be holed up on that side, too. But just to make sure, take fifty men and keep them ready there for emergencies."

When Tim and Diane had left, Governor Slade remained alone in the room with Jimmy. Slade said slowly: "Operator 5, whatever is the result of this fight, I've made costly blunders. I don't deserve the high honor of being Governor of New York. I'm going to resign."

"Don't you do it, Governor," Jimmy urged. "You're honest and you're patriotic. We need men like you for the work ahead of us—reconstruction, rebuilding our institutions and our resources. Forget what's past. If we drive these savages from New York, there'll be plenty of work for you to do in the fields of civil government. And as far as the military blunders you've made, those are between you and me. No one need know of them. It won't do any good to talk about them."

Slade looked at him almost unbelievingly. "You—you mean that? You don't bear me any ill will—"

Jimmy smiled sympathetically. "Ill will? Why should I? Whatever you did was done with honest intention." He stretched out his hand, took Slade's, and shook it. "To the future!" he said.

Slade's eyes glistened. "To the future!" he said.

Jimmy left him standing there, and hurried downstairs into the hall where Flanagan had set up the two hose lines.

DOWN IN the broad foyer of the Post Office Building, everything was set for the reception of the Goths. Flanagan's crew of men were ready with their two lines of hose, and the fifty riflemen whom Jimmy had ordered down there were stationed along the post office windows facing the doors.

From where he stood, Jimmy could see that the flames outside were dying down, and that the boardings were entirely burned away. The glass in the doors themselves had all been smashed in some previous attack upon the building, and there was nothing now to stop the charge of the Goths.

Jimmy peered out into the street, seeking to catch a glimpse of Urslup the Strong, but the Gothic chieftain was nowhere in sight.

And now, with a great shout, the Goths came charging up

the steps of the portico toward the doors. They came from two angles, leaving the center to a group of Gothic riflemen who knelt and raised their rifles to send a volley into the building ahead of their charging comrades.

Jimmy saw the maneuver, and raised his hand to his fifty riflemen. "Fire!"

The fifty riflemen fired as one man, and their volley tore through the kneeling Gothic sharpshooters, mowing them down. The Gothic volley was never fired.

And now, the Gothic infantry were up on the portico, streaming in through the center doors. They were uttering their savage battle cries, brandishing sabres and bayoneted rifles. There were fully three hundred men in that first wave, and they would have been enough to overwhelm the hundred and fifty-odd American defenders.

They were all huge men, cruel fighters, who never gave quarter. And as they streamed into the lobby they seemed to be a terrifying horde.

Jimmy Christopher raised the whistle to his lips, blew four long blasts, and three short ones.

Immediately, the men at the hose opened their nozzles, and two streams of scalding water leaped out at the Gothic attackers. The sizzling water sent up dense clouds of steam, and the battle cries of the Goths turned into cries of agony as the boiling water scalded their flesh, smashing into their faces and legs with pitiless accuracy.

The first wave of those Goths turned desperately to avoid the scalding liquid, and pressed against those behind, trying to get out. Many of them, blinded, threw down their weapons and ran about aimlessly, with their hands before their eyes.

And now, the riflemen at the post office windows, at a signal from Jimmy, raised their guns and sent volley after volley into the thickly pressed throng of savage warriors.

The Goths fell like chaff before the wind, and their victorious charge was converted into a rout. They turned, streaming out of the building, screaming with pain, and leaving their scalded, wounded and dead behind them.

Jimmy motioned to Flanagan, and the hose crew advanced, carrying their lines with them, until they stood on the portico. They continued to spray the street with the hot water, sending the twin streams out into the massed ranks of the second group of Goths, who were to have constituted the second wave of the charge.

These, partly demoralized by the rout of their comrades, broke ranks and turned to run toward the shelter of Pennsylvania Station, across the street.

Urslup the Strong appeared from among a group of his warriors. He was waving his huge mace above his head angrily, and shouting to his men in the guttural language which they used. The men halted in their flight, turned slowly to re-form their ranks, out of reach of the two streams of hot water.

Jimmy motioned to Flanagan once more, and the water was shut off, the hose crew carrying their lines back into the building.

Operator 5 stepped out onto the portico, and looked down the avenue. He uttered a glad cry as he saw a column of Americans, with a color-bearer carrying the Stars and Stripes, coming down the street at the double-quick.

At their head marched old John Court, and behind him came old men, carrying muskets, ancient sabers, pieces of iron pipe—in fact, any kind of weapon that they had been able to lay their hands on.

Jimmy shouted, "Attaboy!"

He could not possibly be heard by Court's column, but the old man had seen him on the portico, and saluted with the sword he was carrying.

NOW THE column of old men struck the rear of the Gothic troops, and the savage warriors turned to meet the new menace that had suddenly appeared at their rear. Their flashing bayonets and curved sabers hacked and stabbed at the elderly attackers, but Court's old men fought with a reckless abandon that has seldom been equaled. They were old, they had been rejected as unfit for service, and now Operator 5 had given them a chance to prove that they were not unfit.

They were intent on making good, and they did. Their old muskets, used as clubs because of lack of ammunition, smashed down upon the skulls of Goths with driving, killing force; their rusty bayonets snapped into the vitals of the savage fighters, and their old lead pipes warded off bayonet thrust and saber slash.

Many of them died in that fight, but it must be marked down with all respect to John Court's brigade, that more Goths died.

And now Jimmy Christopher gave the signal to his own men, and the fifty riflemen, augmented by another eighty who had come from every part of the building, charged out into the street, bayonets flashing, to engage the Goths in hand-to-hand combat.

Taken from both front and rear, the Goths fought savagely, secure in the fact that they outnumbered the Americans. Already more than fifteen hundred had landed. But there were no more than eight or nine hundred here in the street, because the men whom Jimmy had ordered up from the Drive were in the streets west of the post office, sniping from cellars and hastily thrown-up barricades, and preventing the rest of the Goths from coming up from the river.

Jimmy Christopher picked up an empty rifle in the street, and led the charge of the riflemen from the building. With the withdrawal of the two lines of hose, many of the Goths had moved forward again, toward the post office building. Urslup the Strong was a clever and quick-witted general. He had seen at a glance how the trap had been laid for him by Operator 5, and he immediately took steps to meet it.

His orders, barked out in short, guttural phrases, divided his men in two groups of equal size, one group fighting Court's brigade, while the other formed in solid phalanx to meet Jimmy Christopher's riflemen.

Now, when the fate of the battle hung in the balance, Urslup the Strong did not seek the protection of his ring of warriors. He led the second group himself, across Eighth Avenue, which was littered, in front of the post office, with the bodies of dead and wounded Goths, and of scalded men whose shrieks of agony mingled with the desperate shouts of battle and the clashing of steel.

Urslup the Strong was a cruel, merciless, savage chieftain; but no one can deny that he was also a brave man. His mace swung up and down in rhythmic sway as its shining edge smote at American riflemen. Those in the street spread out before that advancing phalanx, to leave room for the charge of Operator 5's riflemen from within the building.

Jimmy Christopher, using his empty rifle as a club, leaped from the portico, with the Americans close behind him, in a sort of wedge of which Jimmy was the apex.

Urslup the Strong saw Operator 5, and though he may not have recognized him, he could see that Jimmy was the leader of the Americans.

He uttered a shout, deep in his throat, and his broad mouth split into a wicked grin of self-assured strength. He headed straight for Jimmy, with his broad mace swinging in the air, whistling as it swished under his powerful hands.

Jimmy Christopher, silent, grim-lipped, strode forward to meet him, and for a while there was a lull in the battle as the Goths and the Americans saw their leaders clash in hand-to-hand combat.

CHAPTER 12
BATTLE OF THE GIANTS

I T WAS like some giant battle of days gone by, when two opposing hosts had suspended hostilities on the field while their chiefs fought to the death for personal prestige. The Goths had seen many an encounter like this one, in which their chief had invariably been victorious. No man, they considered, could stand against the supreme strength and overpowering brawn of Urslup the Strong. They had seen him cleave open a man's skull with one blow of that dreadful mace, and spit him with his long sword, running him through and through with a single thrust. They had no fears as to the outcome of this encounter, and were glad to see it take place, for they expected that the morale of the Americans would be shattered when their leader fell, just as had happened in many another case.

To the strength of their chieftain they owed many a victory. It was their tactics to wait until Urslup the Strong had delivered the mortal blow. Then, when the enemy was still stunned by the loss of its leader, they would utter their savage battle cries, and charge thunderously, taking the enemy at a time when its resistance would be weakest, and slaughtering to their hearts' content.

So they were content to wait the outcome of this hand-to-hand encounter—this deadly duel between their two chiefs.

And if the Americans doubted the outcome of the battle, seeing the immense stature and the rippling muscles of Urslup the Strong, under his leathern armor, they still allowed Operator 5 to do what he wished. He had thus far successfully handled this battle, and they considered that he was entitled to do whatever he deemed fit.

So, the two sides watched while Urslup the Strong, uttering a wild shout of victory, rushed in at Operator 5.

The Gothic chieftain raised his mace high in the air, gripping it with both hands, and brought it down in a blow that seemed to be intended to crush Jimmy Christopher's skull like an eggshell.

Jimmy's narrowed eyes were upon the red-rimmed eyes of Urslup. He did not follow the movement of that murderous mace; rather, he followed his opponent's eyes, as a skillful fencer does.

The spectators expected Operator 5 to attempt to parry the blow with his rifle, and they also expected to see the rifle smashed under the fierce impact of the mace.

But Jimmy Christopher saw Urslup's quick shift of eye, and he stepped back just in time. For instead of bringing the weapon down, Urslup sidestepped cunningly, and swung the mace around in an arc to the right—then slashed with its keen edge at Jimmy's waist.

If Jimmy Christopher had not stepped back with the nimble agility of a trained fencer, that mace would have virtually cut him in half. As it was, it cut through empty air with a wicked, *swishing* sound, like the sound of a snake whip; and Urslup was carried halfway around by its momentum.

He was off balance at the moment, and Jimmy took swift advantage, shortened his rifle, and jabbed the barrel of it into the Gothic chieftain's side. It was not a powerful thrust, for Jimmy, himself, had not had time to set himself after his quick step backward; but it was powerful enough to draw a grunt of pain from Urslup the Strong.

The Americans uttered a low cheer, and the Goths howled with rage.

Urslup backed away, half crouching, swinging the mace with

his left hand while he held his right to his side. He was evidently in pain, but Jimmy could tell by the crafty look in his eyes that he was not seriously disabled.

He circled Jimmy slowly, and Jimmy clubbed his rifle, holding it by the barrel, raised it threateningly. At once Urslup's mace came up in a swift parrying blow, and Jimmy lowered his rifle, changing his stance for a thrust instead of a downswing. But Urslup swung his mace forward and down in a sharp swish, parried the thrust, almost knocking the rifle from Jimmy's grip.

He retained his hold on the rifle, but his hand tingled. He saw now that Urslup's prowess had not been overrated. He was a master of the weapon he carried, and it was no wonder that he had defeated innumerable opponents. Jimmy also remembered that Urslup was said to be as expert with the long sword he carried at his sides as with the mace.

Urslup's thick lips were twisted in a grimace of hate, and his eyes glowed red with spite. He took a quick step forward, and the huge mace came up high over his head. This time, Jimmy knew, he intended to chop down in an effort to crush his skull.

Jimmy raised the rifle, gripping it high in both hands, one hand on the barrel, the other on the stock, holding it horizontal to meet the downswing of the mace.

The mace crashed down upon the rifle, splitting it in two as if it had been a thin stick. The blow was parried. But Jimmy's arms tingled with the impact, and he could feel the shock in his shoulder blades. Urslup's mace flew out of his hands, went spinning into the air twenty feet from where they fought.

Jimmy was left with the two halves of the rifle, while Urslup, stepping back a pace with a wicked grin, drew the long sword from the scabbard at his side!

JIMMY THREW away one broken half of the rifle, retaining the long barrel part. His eyes darted around desperately, spotted a rusty bayonet lying on the ground, where it had doubtless been dropped by a wounded soldier. He leaped toward it, snatched it up just as Urslup uttered another wild yell and ran at him, sword out for a killing thrust into the stomach.

Jimmy Christopher sidestepped that thrust with only a fraction of an inch to spare. The long sword swished by him, and Urslup's huge form reeled close as he followed up the thrust. Jimmy had the broken rifle in one hand, the bayonet in the other. He raised the bayonet, holding it like a dagger, and Urslup, seeing his danger, dropped to the ground, rolled over and over away from him. Then he sprang nimbly to his feet, sword still in hand, and faced Operator 5. Red hate stared out from his eyes. No opponent had ever taken this long to kill or seriously jeopardized his life. Now he circled, with his sword outthrust, seeking an opening.

Jimmy Christopher had seized the opportunity to fit the bayonet into his broken half of the rifle. He now had a passable sword, not quite as long as Urslup's, and without a guard. But he made it serve.

Urslup saw the ridiculous weapon opposed to him, and grinned wickedly. He stepped forward, his sword moving with the swiftness of a serpent, darting in and out dazzlingly.

Jimmy Christopher met every movement of that long sword, parried every thrust, guessed every feint. Operator 5 had studied fencing under the greatest masters of the *épée*. He was a graduate of the *Salle d'Armes* of Scherevesky, the greatest master, then living, of the fencing foils. Though his work in the Intelligence Service had prevented him from entering any of the major European fencing tournaments, Scherevesky, himself, had often told him that he could defeat any champion whom he desired to meet.

The handicap under which he now labored was no greater than many that he had overcome in the past, except for the fact that he was here opposed to a powerful man who did not weaken, and who had apparently also made himself a master of the sword. But what Jimmy Christopher may have lacked in strength, in comparison to Urslup the Strong, he made up in his agility and fine coördination.

His uncouth weapon was everywhere, meeting the blade of Urslup on an equal footing, as if it had been truly a sword and not a makeshift weapon without even a guard.

Urslup was growing angrier every instant, with the blind rage of the wild beast who finds himself balked of his prey; while

Operator 5 retained that coolness which never deserted him even in the face of the greatest emergency.

The Gothic chieftain was anxious to make an end of this combat. He saw his prestige among his own men weakening, and he wished to finish the fight in a spectacular fashion. His thick lips came together in an ominous line, and his eyes grew veiled. Jimmy knew that the vital moment had come, and his body tensed, corded muscles tautening to meet the attack.

Urslup feinted in *tierce*, but Jimmy did not take the bait. He merely seemed to follow the half-thrust, and was ready for the wicked lunge in *seconde* which at once followed it. His bayoneted bit of rifle parried the lunge, sending Urslup's sword wide, and the Goth was left open.

Grimly, Jimmy Christopher set his whole body behind the thrust that caught Urslup in the throat, piercing through to the big man's collarbone.

Urslup uttered a gurgling shriek, and threw up his hands. He staggered a moment as the life blood poured from his throat, then collapsed to the ground, writhing in agony. He threshed on the ground for an instant, and then he lay still.

Urslup the Strong was dead!

The Goths set up shrieks of rage as their chieftain fell, and the Americans began to cheer. Jimmy Christopher had drawn his uncouth sword from Urslup's throat. Now he raised it in the air, and shouted, "At them, boys!"

The Americans responded with a wild cheer, and surged forward against the stunned Gothic troops.

The battle had been raging up the street all this time, with the old men of Court's brigade fighting desperately, hand-to-hand with the second group of Goths, while the American riflemen, barricaded in the streets leading to the river, had been holding back the balance of the landing party of savage warriors.

Now, with the renewed attack of Jimmy's riflemen, the Goths in the street in front of the post office began to fall back, and word spread that Urslup the Strong was dead.

That news seemed to take the starch out of the Gothic fighters. They began to fall back in disorder, apparently seeking only to board their ships once more. Leaderless, they milled about without direction, and the Americans surged in among them, slashing with sword, thrusting with bayonet, giving them no more quarter than they had offered to thousands of American men and women in the past. Perhaps these American riflemen remembered the raids of the last few weeks, where men had been slain, and women had been killed, or raped, or dragged off to the lairs of the Gothic savages.

It was a bloody twenty minutes work, and Jimmy Christopher did not attempt to stop his men, nor the men of Court's brigade, who were fighting like devils incarnate.

Less than half of those Goths managed to reach the safety of their ships, and the streets were strewn with their dead.*

* AUTHOR'S NOTE: Harrison Stievers, the authoritative historian of this period, gives the figures for this engagement, and they may be accepted as authentic. He says, in his monumental history of the Purple Invasion, that no less than four hundred and fifty of the Goths died in the battle, and that no wounded were taken. There were nineteen casualties among Operator

CHAPTER 13
"WE MUST FIGHT AGAIN!"

JIMMY CHRISTOPHER stood in the street, holding his broken rifle with the bayonet attached to it. He watched the rout of the Goths, looking down along Thirty-Third Street, where he had a clear view to the river. His riflemen and Court's Brigade had been joined by the other American troops from the barricades, and they were pushing the retreating Goths, harrying them as they hurried into their boats.

The boats put off from shore as fast as they could, limping back to the Palisades with their defeated, disheartened warriors. The backbone of the Goths was broken. It would now be comparatively easy for Killingsley's men, on the Jersey side, to clean them out of their hiding places, and to free New York for good of their menace.

Jimmy Christopher was tired, spent by the exertion of the last hour, following so hard upon his cross-country journey. He wanted rest above all else—rest and sleep.

A courier came riding down Eighth Avenue, saw him, and dismounted. "Respects of Lieutenant Ferrara, sir," he said, salut-

5's riflemen from the Post Office Building, ans thirty-eight killed and forty wounded among the old men of John Court's brigade. The fight is all the more remarkable, as Stievers notes, by reason of the fact that there were only a total of four hundred and fifty Americans, while the Goths, including those who had landed but did not take part in this fight, numbered sixteen hundred.

ing. "The lieutenant wishes to report that we have defeated the Gothic landing party at Riverside Drive. Hundreds of them are killed, and the others leaped into the river and are swimming to their boats!"

Operator 5 nodded. "My compliments to Lieutenant Ferrara," he said wearily, "and tell him that he helped to save the city. Ask him to report to me in person tomorrow."

As Jimmy turned away from the courier, the jubilant Americans who had remained in the street came thronging around him, cheering, patting him on the back.

Jimmy smiled at the praise, started to make his way back toward the Post Office Building. But he stopped, staring, with a chill feeling of apprehension as he saw two figures come out of the building, running toward him. They were Diane Elliot and Tim Donovan. Diane, he could see, had had her injured wrist strapped up. Tim Donovan was clutching tightly two sheets of paper, and the lad's face was pale, full of concern.

Tim came up to him, forced a smile. "That was a good fight, Jimmy. We sure licked them, didn't we?"

There was a false note in the boy's voice, and Jimmy, who knew him so well that he could recognize any mood of the lad's, detected it instantly.

"What's wrong, Tim?" he demanded.

The boy hesitated, and silently extended the two sheets of paper. "These messages just came in on the heliograph. I—I hated to give them to you now. You must be tired. But I guess you ought to see them."

Diane Elliot came around and put her good hand on Operator 5's shoulder. "It's bad news, Jimmy. Very bad."

Silently, he took the two messages from Tim, and read the first. It was short, terse—

OPERATOR 5. NEW YORK
VIA HELIOGRAPH.
  SHAN HI MUNG'S TROOPS OVERWHELMINGLY
NUMEROUS. GENERAL MALCOLM DEFEATED.
CONTINENTAL CONGRESS DISPERSED. PRES-
IDENT SHERIDAN BARELY ESCAPED WITH HIS
LIFE HIDING IN MICHIGAN. SHAN HI MUNG
WITH SIX DIVISIONS MONGOL TROOPS MARCH-
ING EAST TO NEW YORK.
                    NAN CHRISTOPHER

Operator 5 looked up from the message, to meet the eyes of Diane and Tim fixed upon him. His voice was a bit hoarse as he asked, "The—the other message—it's bad news also?"

Tim Donovan gulped, and nodded. Jimmy let his eyes drop to the second one—

GOVERNOR SLADE. NEW YORK.
VIA HELIOGRAPH FROM RICHMOND, VA.
  PURPLE FLEET SHELLED CHARLESTON TODAY.
LANDED MARINES AND PUT ALL RESIDENTS TO
THE SWORD. SAILED AWAY AND IS BELIEVED
HEADED FOR NEW YORK. ADVISE YOU EVACU-
ATE AND RETIRE INLAND. IMPOSSIBLE RESIST...

HENRY HELICON,
GOVERNOR OF VIRGINIA

The small group of three was silent for a long minute. Then Jimmy Christopher said bitterly: "So! We use our last ounce of energy to save New York from the Goths, and now we are faced by a double peril—the Purple Fleet from the sea and Shan Hi Mung's Mongols from the west!"

"What are you going to do, Jimmy?" Diane asked.

"Do?" he laughed harshly. "We won't retire inland. We'll make our stand here. We must fight again. Somehow, some way, we must find a means of stopping that fleet—and that horde of murdering Mongols!"

Tim Donovan's eyes shone as he saw the returning vigor in Operator 5. Just a moment ago, after a hard-fought victory, he had been tired, weary, sleepy. Now, with a new threat facing the country, every faculty of his had suddenly come awake, alert. His words were crisp, alive with energy, and he spoke with strong conviction.

"America still has some fight left in her!" he went on. "Come on. We've got to make plans. We've got to organize. When old men like those in Court's brigade can fight the way they did today, we young bloods can't possibly lie down on the job!"

"Attaboy!" said Tim Donovan under his breath, as he followed Operator 5 and Diane Elliot into the Post Office Building. The lad's eyes were shining with courage, and with unswerving confidence that Operator 5 would still find a way out for America!*

* AUTHOR'S NOTE: Harrison Stievers, the well-known historian of this period, gives us a very prosaic account of the events that occurred when the marching hosts of Shan Hi Mung and the floating fortresses of the Purple Fleet under Admiral von der Selz converged upon New York. Many people have found fault with the way in which Stievers treats this phase of America's struggle for existence, when President Sheridan attempted to coördinate that Government of the United States from a barn in Michigan, and Operator 5 attempted to save New York from the double peril which assailed it. This prosaic treatment on Stievers' part, however, is not due to the eminent historian's lack of enthusiasm, but to his lack of information. In subsequent chronicles, I shall lean heavily upon the personal notes of Operator 5 and of Diane Elliot and Nan Christopher, and it will become apparent that some of the most thrilling episodes of the Purple Invasion took place at this time.

POPULAR HERO PULPS AVAILABLE NOW:

THE SPIDER

- ❏ #1: The Spider Strikes — $13.95
- ❏ #2: The Wheel of Death — $13.95
- ❏ #3: Wings of the Black Death — $13.95
- ❏ #4: City of Flaming Shadows — $13.95
- ❏ #5: Empire of Doom! — $13.95
- ❏ #6: Citadel of Hell — $13.95
- ❏ #7: The Serpent of Destruction — $13.95
- ❏ #8: The Mad Horde — $13.95
- ❏ #9: Satan's Death Blast — $13.95
- ❏ #10: The Corpse Cargo — $13.95
- ❏ #11: Prince of the Red Looters — $13.95
- ❏ #12: Reign of the Silver Terror — $13.95
- ❏ #13: Builders of the Dark Empire — $13.95
- ❏ #14: Death's Crimson Juggernaut — $13.95
- ❏ #15: The Red Death Rain — $13.95
- ❏ #16: The City Destroyer — $13.95
- ❏ #17: The Pain Emperor — $13.95
- ❏ #18: The Flame Master — $13.95
- ❏ #19: Slaves of the Crime Master — $13.95
- ❏ #20: Reign of the Death Fiddler — $13.95
- ❏ #21: Hordes of the Red Butcher — $13.95
- ❏ #22: Dragon Lord of the Underworld — $13.95
- ❏ #23: Master of the Death-Madness — $13.95
- ❏ #24: King of the Red Killers — $13.95
- ❏ #25: Overlord of the Damned — $13.95
- ❏ #26: Death Reign of the Vampire King — $13.95
- ❏ #27: Emperor of the Yellow Death — $13.95
- ❏ #28: The Mayor of Hell — $13.95
- ❏ #29: Slaves of the Murder Syndicate — $13.95
- ❏ #30: Green Globes of Death — $13.95
- ❏ #31: The Cholera King — $13.95
- ❏ #32: Slaves of the Dragon — $13.95
- ❏ #33: Legions of Madness — $12.95
- ❏ #34: Laboratory of the Damned — $12.95
- ❏ #35: Satan's Sightless Legion — $12.95
- ❏ #36: The Coming of the Terror — $12.95
- ❏ #37: The Devil's Death-Dwarfs — $12.95
- ❏ #38: City of Dreadful Night — $12.95
- ❏ #39: Reign of the Snake Men — $12.95
- ❏ #40: Dictator of the Damned — $12.95
- ❏ #41: The Mill-Town Massacres — $12.95
- ❏ #42: Satan's Workshop — $12.95
- ❏ #43: Scourge of the Yellow Fangs — $12.95
- ❏ #44: The Devil's Pawnbroker — $12.95
- ❏ #45: Voyage of the Coffin Ship — $12.95
- ❏ #46: The Man Who Ruled in Hell — $13.95
- ❏ #47: Slaves of the Black Monarch — $13.95
- ❏ #48: Machineguns Over the White House — $13.95
- ❏ #49: The City That Dared Not Eat — $13.95
- ❏ #50: Master of the Flaming Horde — $13.95
- ❏ #51: Satan's Switchboard — $13.95
- ❏ #52: Legions of the Accursed Light — $13.95
- ❏ #53: The City of Lost Men — $13.95
- ❏ #54: The Grey Horde Creeps — $13.95
- ❏ #55: City of Whispering Death — $13.95
- ❏ #56: When Thousands Slept in Hell — $13.95
- ❏ #57: Satan's Shakles — $14.95
- ❏ #58: The Emperor From Hell — $14.95
- ❏ #59: The Devil's Candlesticks — $14.95
- ❏ #60: The City That Paid to Die — $14.95
- ❏ #61: The Spider at Bay — $14.95
- ❏ #62: Scourge of the Black Legions — $14.95
- ❏ #63: The Withering Death — $14.95
- ❏ #64: Claws of the Golden Dragon — $14.95
- ❏ **NEW:** #65: The Song of Death — $14.95

THE WESTERN RAIDER

- ❏ #1: Guns of the Damned — $13.95
- ❏ #2: The Hawk Rides Back from Death — $13.95
- ❏ #3: Gun-Call for the Lost Legion — $13.95
- ❏ #4: The Law of Silver Trent — $13.95
- ❏ #5: The Gun-Prayer of Silver Trent — $13.95
- ❏ #6: Silver Trent Rides Alone — $13.95

G-8 AND HIS BATTLE ACES

- ❏ #1: The Bat Staffel — $13.95

CAPTAIN SATAN

- ❏ #1: The Mask of the Damned — $13.95
- ❏ #2: Parole for the Dead — $13.95
- ❏ #3: The Dead Man Express — $13.95
- ❏ #4: A Ghost Rides the Dawn — $13.95
- ❏ #5: The Ambassador From Hell — $13.95

DR. YEN SIN

- ❏ #1: Mystery of the Dragon's Shadow — $12.95
- ❏ #2: Mystery of the Golden Skull — $12.95
- ❏ #3: Mystery of the Singing Mummies — $12.95